A Bakery Called Scrumptious

DeVon Nelson

Library of Congress Control Number TXu2-175-092

ISBN 978-0-578-68715-5

Printed in the United States of America

First Edition

ACKNOWLEDGMENTS

This book wouldn't have been possible without so many people. I wish to acknowledge the invaluable help of my editors, Brian Paone, Danielle Huffman-Hanni, and Elaina Robbins.

Special thanks to Rose Miller for designing my peachy book cover.

I'm especially grateful to my family and friends for listening to me during my many brainstorming sessions.

I thank my readers for reading my books and helping me grow as a writer.

And most of all, I thank my Lord and Savior for encouraging me when I wanted to quit, strengthening me after a night of writing, and then having to go to work, and for gifting me with calm when my thoughts were in angst.

I'm dedicating this book to all the dreamers — whether your heart is set on opening a bakery, becoming a writer, or finishing a 5k race — You can do it!

To quote Maya Angelou "Life loves to be taken by the lapel and told: 'I'm with you kid. Let's go.'"

CHAPTER ONE

Bakery

A large pink and white "Home Sweet Home" banner hung outside 1202 Wentworth Lane, a modest home in a quiet neighborhood of cul-de-sacs and tree-lined streets. Inside, big balloons in various shades of purple—Shianne's favorite color—filled the entryway. Chocolate, strawberry, and lemon cupcakes rested on a coffee table.

"Where are they?" Michelle asked, peeking out the living room window. "They should have been here an hour ago."

"Your guess is as good as mine," Erica said. "Knowing Shianne, they stopped off at a store somewhere." Erica shifted her leggy body on the cream sofa as her eyes fixed on a crystal pendant chandelier. "This house is beautiful. It's *so*, Shianne."

Michelle bit into a cupcake and plunked onto a purple armchair. "It is beautiful, all right."

Cream-colored floral wallpaper with geometric circles contrasting with vibrant purple curtains and modern furniture and lighting created a chic ambiance to the living room space.

"That girl forever amazes me. She wasn't here half of the time, and still managed to decorate the house amazingly," Michelle said.

Erica nodded. "That's Shianne. She can make things happen from anywhere."

Shianne and Gregory White had purchased the four-bedroom brick home a few months after Gregory's job transferred to Chicago.

Having to start work immediately, Gregory had moved into the house without Shianne and Kaiya, their five-year-old daughter. They had remained in St. Louis, Missouri, packing for the move.

Moments later, Michelle and Erica heard car doors banging. Michelle's deep brown eyes widened in anticipation as she ran to a window and peeked. "They're here!"

"About time," Erica said, hopping off the sofa and running over next to her.

They listened for the door to unlock, and as soon as Shianne entered, they yelled, "Surprise!" Erica blew a party favor as Michelle threw confetti into the air.

Shianne smiled wildly.

"Welcome home," Michelle said, hugging her. "I've missed you so much."

"I've missed you too. It doesn't seem like I was here just a few weeks ago."

"It seems longer. You look great," Michelle continued.

Shianne's bronze face glowed radiantly as her lengthy black hair rested nicely on her shoulders. Michelle had long admired Shianne's hair. She could whip it into any style she chose to wear—curly, up in a ponytail, or straight.

"What about me?" Erica said.

Shianne reached over and hugged her. "I've missed you too." Shianne gave Erica's hair a second look. "I like the new 'do.'"

Erica pressed her hand against the back of her short haircut and ran her fingers through the top, fluffing it up.

"Short hair looks good on you. When did you get rid of your braids?"

"A week ago. I've worn braids for as long as you've known me. I wanted to try something different, something a little more daring."

Michelle laughed. "Girl, the new man in her life has her changing hairstyles as much as she changes her lipstick."

Shianne grinned. "Oh, is Aaron the reason for this? Well, whatever the reason, it's adorable. You look like you're in your twenties again."

"Well thank you," said Erica, who was in her mid-thirties.

"Michelle and I were just adoring your house. It's lovely," Erica continued.

Shianne set her designer purse on the sofa and smiled. "Gregory and I decided to have the flooring and walls finished before Ki and I moved in. Have you seen her cute little pink bedroom?"

"Yes, it's so cute."

As they were talking, Kaiya entered the room, her long ponytail bouncing. All eyes turned on her.

"Baby girl, if you don't look like your mother," Michelle said, smiling.

"Doesn't she," Erica echoed. "Little mama is so cute."

"Come give your aunties a hug," Michelle said, stretching her arms ready for a hug. "We've missed you."

Kaiya walked over and hugged the two.

Moments later, Gregory, a light-skinned man of average height, carried two suitcases inside the room and dropped them in the middle of the floor. He shook his head. "What do you have in these suitcases, Shianne?"

Shianne grinned. "Sugar, spice, and all things nice. I'll show you tonight," she said, winking.

"Let's eat," Michelle said. "It's getting X-rated in here."

"Sounds good to me," Gregory said. "Ki, go wash your hands."

Michelle and Erica put the food on the table while the others washed for dinner. Moments later, Shianne walked into the dining room and gave a loud gasp.

"Our housewarming gifts to the family," Michelle said.

A centerpiece of fresh, long-stemmed flowers and a set of Waterford Crystal dinnerware donned the glass dining table.

"Oh, it's so pretty. I love it! Thank you, ladies," she said, taking a seat at the table.

"Gregory, would you bless the food please?" Shianne asked.

Moments later, forks and spoons clanged against the plates as they dug into a tossed salad, salmon croquettes, brown rice, and vegetables.

Shianne raised her glass of tea in the air. "Kudos to the chefs. The salmon croquettes are delicious. They're almost as good as mine."

Michelle grinned. "They *are* yours. I used your recipe." She pulled a stained, folded piece of paper from her jeans pocket and waved it in the air.

"Is that Grandma Eva's salmon recipe?" Shianne asked excitedly.

Michelle nodded. "Yes."

Shianne's eyes narrowed. "You had the recipe? No wonder I couldn't find it."

Michelle handed it to her. "Remember, I borrowed it when I made salmon croquettes for Dad's fifty-seventh birthday."

"That was two years ago!" She paused. "Are those egg and onion stains on it?" Shianne held up the recipe for everyone to see. "Looks like you've used it quite a bit."

"I've used it a few times."

"A few times?" Shianne repeated, laughing. "I'm putting it back in my recipe book with the others—onion stains and all."

"I'm sure you have the recipe memorized by now," Michelle said.

"Aw, sweet," Erica said. "Let's toast to your new home and to recovering Grandma Eva's missing salmon recipe."

"Cheers," everyone said, including Kaiya, who raised her glass of apple juice.

Shianne stared at the crinkled piece of paper for a few moments and placed it next to her plate. "Speaking of cooking, I talked with Chef Brown a few days ago. He's retired from the restaurant and is looking forward to moving back to Chicago with his family. He's willing to work with me at the bakery."

"Terrific," Michelle said. "He'll be a big help to you. He has so much experience."

Chef Brown and Shianne had befriended each other at a baker's convention in New York one summer. They had hit it off instantly, conversing like old friends during the weekend of confectionary heaven. Their friendship had continued afterward through occasional telephone calls.

"When do you plan to open it?" Erica asked.

"I'm hoping in a few months," Shianne said, not taking her eyes off her plate. "The space on Sheffield is still available. I talked with the owner last week." Gregory's head jerked in her direction. "I'm talking about the place in Evanston that Michelle and I looked at last month."

"You never mentioned a place." He raised an eyebrow. "This is my first time hearing about it."

She cocked her head to the side. "No, it isn't. Remember, we talked about it at dinner one night. I talked about hanging a pink and purple awning on the outside."

With a look of bewilderment, he said, "No, I don't remember. And why, Evanston? Why not here in Schaumburg?"

Shianne's brow furrowed. "I'm familiar with Evanston. I have a lot of friends there who'll support the bakery. It's also a nice city to open a business."

"And so is Schaumburg."

For a quick moment, Shianne wondered if she had forgotten to tell Gregory but remembered she had. He was favorable toward Evanston as a possible site for the bakery.

Kaiya's fork dropped in her plate, making a loud clanging sound. Everyone turned to her. "Mommy, I finished my dinner," she said, displaying a missing bottom tooth. "Can I have a cupcake?"

Gregory frowned. "You had a brownie earlier, Kaiya. No."

Shianne touched his arm. "Let her have half a cupcake. We're celebrating our homecoming."

He sighed. "Okay, just half."

Kaiya smiled and left the room.

The group continued eating and talking, refraining from anything remotely connected to the bakery. Shortly after, Michelle and Erica put away the leftovers and cleaned the kitchen before saying goodnight.

"I hope everything's all right," Erica said, climbing into Michelle's car. "Gregory seemed a little bothered. No, he was pissed. Something tells me they'll talk about the bakery late into the night."

Michelle sighed. "Too bad. Shianne and Gregory should be having hot, steamy, homecoming sex tonight."

Shianne helped Kaiya get ready for bed, then got ready for bed herself. She'd planned a romantic evening with Gregory, starting with a warm bath. When she entered the bathroom, Gregory was in his pajama bottoms and brushing his teeth. She wrapped her arms around his waist and kissed him on the neck. "It feels good being home, honey. I missed not having you around; I don't like the nights without you."

"Yep," he said distantly and wiped his mouth with a washcloth.

She withdrew her arms from his waist, disrobed, and stepped into the shower. Shianne thought her naked body would entice him to join her, but he walked out of the bathroom and into their adjoining bedroom. *Looks like I won't be wearing my cute little nightie tonight.*

The waterfall rain shower felt good touching her body. Shianne closed her eyes and again wondered had she told Gregory about the bakery site. She thought for several moments and was sure she had. She then hoped she and Gregory would end the night romancing instead of him giving her the cold shoulder.

Shianne dried and oiled her body with the sweet-smelling oil Gregory had bought her in New York. She reached for her bathrobe behind the bathroom door but decided against putting it on. Instead, she walked naked into the bedroom.

Gregory was sitting upright, watching TV. He pretended not to see her, but Shianne knew he was watching her every move.

She turned off the TV and climbed into bed, snuggling close to him. "Why are you ignoring me? You're making me think you didn't miss me." She took his hand. "I know we need to talk about some things, Gregory, but right now, I need to make love to my husband. It's been a long two weeks." She gave him a moist kiss on the lips, followed by another.

Gregory locked his arms around her and held her close. "Yes, we need to talk, Shianne."

"Fine, but can we talk in the morning, please?"

Shianne and Gregory were awakened the next morning to Kaiya knocking on the door. "Mommy, I'm hungry. Daddy, can I make my cereal?" she asked through the door.

"Sure, baby," Gregory said, snuggling closer to Shianne. "Mommy and I are getting dressed. We'll be out in a few minutes, okay?"

"Okay."

Gregory and Shianne continued last night's romancing, and when they got downstairs several moments later, Kaiya was in the family room watching TV.

Shianne kissed her on the forehead. "Good morning, my sweetie."

Kaiya pouted. "You took too long." She eyed the fallen Rice Krispies on the floor. "I spilled some of my cereal."

"It's okay," Gregory said. He picked up the cereal and held it in his hand. "Mommy and I fell back asleep. We were tired from the trip."

"Who wants pancakes?" Shianne asked.

"I do, I do," Kaiya said. "Can I help you make them, Mommy?"

"Sure, you can help Mommy. We'll leave Daddy here to watch the news while we make breakfast."

Kaiya took Shianne's hand, and they started for the kitchen. Together they made pancakes—a few teddy bear ones for Kaiya—bacon, and eggs. Afterward, the family went shopping for plants and flowers for their new home.

Shianne made sure not to mention the bakery. They were in too good of a mood.

CHAPTER TWO

Michelle was up to her eyelids with creating new greeting cards when she answered Shianne's angry call. "Cards from the Heart. This is Michelle speaking."

"Come! Get! Me!"

"Where are you?" Michelle asked.

"At home."

Michelle cringed. "What's going on?"

"Girl, Gregory has me so upset. He's all frowned up because he overheard me talking to Chef Brown this morning about the bakery. All I said was I was looking at a site. He took it as if I'd made up my mind and was ready to set up shop. Can you believe him?" She hesitated. "I need some air. Will you pick us up? My car is in the shop."

Michelle knew by Shianne's tone that she was agitated. "Uh, sure. I'm on my way."

As quickly as Michelle clicked off her phone, it rang again. She answered, assuming it was Shianne canceling her mayday call.

"Hey, girl," Erica said.

Michelle took a deep sigh. "Oh, it's you. I thought you were Shianne."

"Why the somber tone? What's going on?"

"She's mad at Greg. She wants to come over for a while."

"They were all lovey-dovey the other day when I ran into them at the store. Let me guess—it's the bakery again?"

"Chef Brown called her this morning, wanting to know how things were going with it. Gregory overheard their conversation and I guess got upset."

"Don't they argue about anything else? This bakery stuff is getting old. He *does* want her to open the bakery, right?"

"Yes, I believe so."

"Then what's the problem?"

"Erica, I don't know. Sheesh!"

"I'm just asking. Don't get mad at me." She sighed. "Pick me up. I'll ride with you."

Uh-oh. Her showing up at Shianne's house was troubling enough, but for Gregory to see Erica tagging along would be disastrous, she thought. But she picked her up anyway.

Thirty minutes later, Gregory opened the door and flinched. "Did Shianne call you over here?"

Before they could answer, Shianne came rushing down the stairs with a large gold leather bag in hand. Kaiya followed with a smaller bag of the same color.

"You going to Michelle's won't solve anything," Gregory said. "We need to talk this out."

"We've been talking about this for the last hour." Shianne retrieved her sweater from the hallway closet.

Gregory faced Michelle and tossed his arms in the air. "I can't reason with her. I don't understand why she's getting all bent out of shape just because I said we need to do more planning with the bakery. She's not being fair."

"We've planned 'till I'm blue in the face, Gregory." She tapped her foot. "Look at my face, girls. What color is it?"

"Really, Shianne? I think you're being a little dramatic," Gregory said, eyeing Erica as if he dared her to say something.

Michelle's heart pounded. *Please, Erica, don't say anything. Please!*
Erica remained quiet.

Whew!

Gregory crossed his arms. "Nothing's wrong with us taking our time to do it right, Shianne."

"I don't mean to get into your business, but I thought the bakery was a go," Erica said.

Gregory's gaze hardened. "You're right. It's none of your business." He faced Shianne. "I give up. Do what you want. Start your business tomorrow if you want. I'll bail you out when you fail."

Shianne winced. Tears filled her eyes as she regarded him with disgust. "I never expected you to say something like that."

Kaiya ran to Shianne and hugged her waist. "Don't cry, Mommy."

Shianne wiped the corner of her eyes, and through trembling lips said, "How many of your businesses have failed? I never once rubbed it in your face. You know why? Because I love you. I had your back. I was with you all the way, regardless of how things turned out."

Gregory had opened a few businesses, including a bar. It had belonged to his cousin, but delinquent taxes had it heading toward foreclosure, so Gregory acquired it. Juggling two jobs proved hard for Gregory, so he sold the bar a year later at no profit. He had also owned a men's clothing store. It had closed after a year too.

Gregory chewed on his bottom lip. Shame filled his eyes.

Shianne knew her unveiling rattled him, but she didn't care. Gregory had embarrassed her in front of her friends. "You used to be my biggest cheerleader. What happened to you?" Shianne marched toward the door. "Come on, Kaiya."

Kaiya ran to her father and hugged him. "See you later, Daddy. I love you. Are you coming to Aunt Michelle's later?"

"Love you too, sweetie," was all he could muster.

Erica followed Shianne and Kaiya.

Michelle wanted to say something to Gregory, but instead gave a sorrowful look and closed the door behind her.

"He makes me so sick sometimes," Shianne said as they got inside the car. "He can be so stubborn."

It was a quiet ride to Michelle's, except for Kaiya singing along to songs on the radio. Shianne didn't want to discuss the matter further around Kaiya.

Shianne was ashamed at the way she and Gregory had argued in front of Kaiya. She finished washing her face, and then entered the bedroom where Kaiya was lying across the bed, watching TV. Shianne sat beside her.

"Hey, baby. I'm sorry about today. You should never have seen your father and I argue the way we did. It should never have happened in front of you."

Kaiya used an elbow to prop her face onto an open palm. "I don't like you and Daddy arguing, Mommy."

"I know, baby. We don't enjoy arguing either." She put her arm around Kaiya and kissed her forehead.

"You can call your father in the morning. He might pick you up from camp tomorrow. I have a meeting, and I don't know if I'll be out in time to get you."

Michelle knocked on the door and entered, smiling. "I made our favorite blueberry pomegranate smoothie." She handed Kaiya the cup.

"Thanks, Aunt Michelle." She took a sip and smiled.

"I have one for you too, Shianne when you come downstairs."

"Thanks. I'll be down in a few."

Michelle then turned to Kaiya. "Goodnight, Kaiya."

"Goodnight, Aunt Michelle."

Fifteen minutes later, Shianne went downstairs to meet with the girls. Michelle was enjoying a smoothie while Erica ate a hearty sandwich of ham, turkey, lettuce, American cheese, and green peppers. Shianne surveyed the sandwich.

"What? I was hungry," Erica said, picking up the sandwich.

"I didn't say anything." Shianne pulled a chair from the table and sat.

"You didn't have to. Your facial expression said it all."

"Well, if you must know, I was thinking you never seem to gain weight as much as you eat."

"I gain weight if I think about food," Michelle chimed in.

"No, you don't," Shianne said. "You're almost the same size you were in college. You may have gained maybe five pounds."

Michelle smiled, knowing she had gained at least ten pounds since college. "Five pounds? I'll take it. Thanks."

They all laughed.

"How's my baby girl?" Erica asked.

Shianne shook her head. "I believe we scared her. I apologized to her and told her not to worry about us."

Erica shivered. "I hated it when my parents argued. It scared the heck out of Audrey and me. We'd hide in our bedroom closet until they stopped. Sometimes we'd fall asleep in there. I remember the first time we hid inside the closet, and they couldn't find us. They searched everywhere for us. Even checked with the neighbors, asking if they'd seen us. Mama checked the closet and found us." She bit into her sandwich and chewed. "They stopped arguing in front of us when Audrey threatened to run away."

"She did?" Shianne asked.

Erica nodded. "She sure did. She told them she would live with Aunt Nancy if they didn't cut it out."

"This was our first argument in front of her. I feel terrible. I never want her to feel frightened by us."

Shianne picked up the newspaper from the table. Flipping through the sports pages, she came across a story on the Northwestern Panthers and a picture of her old boyfriend, Miles Montgomery. Shianne drew the article closer and read.

Michelle's heart beat fast. She'd planned to put away the newspaper after reading the article, but a telephone call had distracted her, and she forgot about it.

Shianne took a few minutes to read the story and then set it down. Erica's face soured.

"What's on your mind?" Shianne asked, staring at her.

Michelle gave Erica *the look*, the one that said keep your damn mouth closed.

"I don't have anything to say, other than I can't stand his ass."

"How many times have you said this, Erica? I don't care if you like him or not."

"Are you serious?

"Yes. Do you realize how many years it's been since Miles and I broke up?"

"About five, but …"

"But what?"

Erica wiped her mouth with a napkin and studied Shianne's face. "You have his daughter. He cheated on you with his ex-girlfriend."

Shianne grimaced. "I know whose daughter I have. Do you have to remind me every time his name comes up?"

"Erica, be quiet," Michelle said. She knew Shianne was doing everything to keep from cussing Erica out.

Shianne gave a dismissive wave of her hand. "I don't know how many conversations we have to have about this, Erica. I know you don't understand my thinking, but it's not for you to understand. Why does it matter to you so much, anyway? Mind your own business and stop trying to fix mine."

Erica hissed, then pinched a piece off her sandwich and brought it to her mouth and chewed.

Michelle knew by Shianne's peppered speech she was fuming. She questioned why Shianne hadn't mentioned Erica's many troubled relationships—like when she had dated Jimmy, a well-put-together businessman who almost stole thousands of dollars from Erica. And there was Lance, who had pretended his marriage was over but continued living with his wife.

"I'm sorry," Erica said.

"You're always throwing your two cents in when it's not needed," Shianne said.

"I was just—"

Shianne scowled. "Just what? Just shut the hell up, Erica! I'm tired of having these stupid-ass conversations with you." She stormed from the room.

"Good one, Erica," Michelle said. "You know that wasn't cool. Keep your sidebars to yourself. How would you feel if she threw your mistakes or bad relationships in your face all the time?" A muscle in Erica's jaw twitched. "Yes, exactly. Show a little sensitivity."

"Why does she get so weird about this?"

"It's obvious you're not hearing me, Erica," Michelle said flustered. "The man hurt her. He broke her heart. He was her first love. Don't you get it?"

Shianne had met Miles in college and fell madly in love with him. After college, they had discussed getting married, but Miles committed an indiscretion with his high school sweetheart, and he and Shianne broke up. It was after their breakup Shianne had learned she was pregnant and didn't tell Miles.

Erica rolled her eyes and scrunched her face. "I'm not trying to hurt or embarrass her, but she's crazy. She should tell Miles about Kaiya and make him pay child support. He certainly has the money."

"Maybe she doesn't want his money. Did you ever think about that? Gregory is taking excellent care of them. Maybe she doesn't want to have anything to do with Miles. Maybe opening that door again would be too painful."

Erica disregarded the comment. "I don't know why she doesn't."

Michelle closed her eyes in exasperation. "See, this is what I mean. You're hopeless. Aren't you tired of sounding like a broken record?" Michelle left the kitchen, leaving Erica alone.

Shianne was lying on the sofa when Michelle entered the room and sat at the sofa's foot.

Erica walked in moments later and sat in a chair across from Shianne, who gave her a cool look. Feeling Shianne's cold stare, Erica quickly abandoned the seat and sought refuge on the loveseat further away.

"I loved Miles for the longest time after we broke up," Shianne said, breaking the silence. "I wondered if I would ever love another man as much as I loved him. I didn't want to." She faced Erica. "There's a saying, 'You don't know what you had until it's gone, and you don't know what you've been missing until it arrives.' Well, Gregory arrived and showed me I was skimming the surface with Miles. I don't think about Miles. I don't care about what's happening in his life. Do you understand what I'm saying?"

Erica swallowed deep and nodded.

"Sure, I thought about calling Miles plenty of times to tell him about Ki, especially during our lean times. But Mom and Dad and you guys pitched in and helped me whenever I needed it. I didn't need Miles. I was too angry to tell him, anyway. He cheated on me with Brandy. That's a hard pill to swallow. I've forgiven him, but I'll never forget the hurt he caused me."

"That's why he should be paying child support," Erica said, stretching. "It makes me so dang mad when women don't file for child support for their kids. They take the responsibility away from their fathers. Miles had skin in the game when he got you pregnant, Shianne. He should have bands in his hand to help support Kaiya."

"I have no doubt had Miles known about Ki he would have offered to help me with her, and you know it," Shianne said.

Michelle nodded.

"Well, he needs to know, and he's still an ass," Erica said.

Michelle covered her face with her hands and shook her head.

The girls talked late into the night, even belly laughed a few times, before retiring.

Michelle patted a sleeping Erica on the shoulder. "Girl, go to bed. You aren't going home tonight."

Erica stood sluggishly, mumbled a goodnight, and headed upstairs.

"Goodnight, player," Shianne said.

"You're as bad as she is with the sarcasm," Michelle said. "I'm going to bed too. Do you need anything?"

Shianne shook her head and wrapped herself further into the blanket. "No, I'm good. I'm sorry about getting you guys involved in my mess today."

"Don't be sorry. This is what friends do."

Shianne closed her eyes. "I don't know what's happening with Gregory. One moment he's excited about the bakery and giving me ideas, then the next thing I know, he's telling me I should hold off." She shook her head. "I can't deal with his indecisiveness, his flip-flopping. I'm so done! I'm moving on with my plans. When Miles and I broke up, I swore I'd never let another man deter me from what I wanted to do." She gave Michelle a somber expression. "Remember, I had a job in New York waiting for me after college. But, hah, I wanted to stay in Chicago so that I could be close to Miles. Well, I got news for everybody. It's my turn now." Tears welled in her eyes.

Michelle sat beside Shianne and wrapped her arm around her. "You guys will work it out. Gregory will pull through. He loves you too much. You know he won't let his Shi-boo down."

Shianne's mouth curved into a smile. "Goodnight."

Michelle was having the most incredible dream when the need to use the washroom awakened her. *Why does this always happen? I'm dreaming of this tall, handsome man rubbing his hand through my hair, and I have to wake up for a pee break. I should have just peed on myself.*

Michelle thought she would get something to drink afterward. When she went downstairs, Shianne was standing on the patio outside the kitchen. Michelle tapped on the sliding glass door and opened it.

"I love how it smells after a good rainfall," Shianne said.

Michelle inhaled the sweet and crisp air and then scanned the backyard as if she were looking at it for the first time. She'd forgotten how beautiful the yard was. "You know, I haven't spent a lot of time out here since Aunt Vi died."

"I don't know why you haven't. It's beautiful out here. It's so peaceful. You can do a lot of good thinking back here."

Michelle and her Aunt Victoria—called Aunt Vi—had often sat outside before her death. Thoughts of Aunt Vi planting flowers and vegetables in her garden, her favorite straw hat cocked to the side, a red bandana wrapped around her neck, and Ms. Perkins, her Yorkshire terrier, following behind set in her mind. She smiled.

"What are you smiling about?"

"I was thinking about Aunt Vi and Ms. Perkins being out here together. The two were so adorable together. They were inseparable."

Shianne grinned. "I don't know why Ms. Perkins didn't like me. She would snap at me as soon as I stepped in the door."

"Aunt Vi said you did something to her."

Shianne's eyes widened. "I did not. I would never hurt Ms. Perkins for fear that Aunt Vi would hit me with something. Don't tell me Aunt Vi went to the grave, thinking I hit her dog?"

Michelle giggled. "No, that was my thinking."

"Well, since that was your thinking, I hit her across the butt one time with a newspaper."

"You hit Ms. Perkins, for real?"

"I was kidding. But I should have, as much as Ms. Perkins growled at me."

Michelle's eyes narrowed. "You better not have hit my dog."

"Girl, go back to bed. And Ms. Perkins wasn't your dog. See you in the morning."

CHAPTER THREE

Shianne and Kaiya were eating breakfast when Michelle strolled into the kitchen. Shianne had made French banana toast for Kaiya and mini bacon and egg sandwiches for the girls.

"Mm, what smells so good?" Michelle asked, glancing at the stove. "Ooh, Shianne's minis, my favorite."

Michelle pulled a plate from the cabinet and placed three tiny sandwiches on it. She walked over to the table where a bowl of sliced apples, kiwi, and grapes rested. "How long have you guys been up?" she asked, dipping a spoonful of fruit onto her plate before sitting.

"Mommy wakes me up at seven, Aunt Michelle," Kaiya said.

"What time did you get up Shianne?"

"I didn't sleep well. I was up around five and started dinner."

"Dinner?" Erica chimed, joining the girls. "What's for dinner?" She walked over to the counter and poured herself a cup of coffee.

"We're having teriyaki chicken kebabs with my special dipping sauce, coconut rice, grilled vegetables, and avocado salad."

"Yucky," Kaiya interrupted.

"For dessert, we'll have raspberries and whipped cream."

"Mm, I love raspberries," Kaiya said.

"So do I," Erica said, gazing at the small sandwiches on the stove. "Look at the cute little sandwiches. I love applewood bacon." She picked up a sandwich and bit into it. "I'll take a few of these with me. I have to go home and get dressed. I'm showing a house this morning." Erica wrapped the sandwiches and waved. "I'll see everyone tonight."

"Who invited you?" Michelle asked.

"I invited myself." She faced Shianne. "I'm sorry I can't make it to the inspection, but I'm here for you. Whatever you need, ask."

"Thanks. I appreciate the offer."

"Goodbye, Aunt Erica," Kaiya said.

"Have a great day, baby."

Shianne drew her coffee to her mouth and took a sip. "We should get moving too, Ki. Finish eating your food."

Kaiya popped the last piece of toast into her mouth. "Finished! I'll get my bookbag."

Michelle smiled. "She is quite a little lady. I know I don't have to tell you, but you guys are doing a great job with her."

"Thanks." She paused. "You're coming this afternoon, right?"

"Gregory's not going with you?" Michelle asked, thinking his opinion mattered more than hers, being he was the husband and financial partner.

Shianne shrugged. "I don't know. He knows about it." She stared at Michelle as she waited for an answer.

Michelle swallowed hard. "Yes, sure. I have a meeting late morning, but I'll be there."

Shianne had looked over much of the store space by the time Michelle arrived.

"I'm sorry, I'm late. My meeting went a little long."

"No problem, as long as you sealed the deal."

"It looks very promising. How are things here?"

"Good." She turned to the building owner. "Max, you remember Michelle?"

"Sure, I do." The red-haired man shook her hand. "I was showing Shianne some updates we've made since you were last here."

Moments later, Gregory rushed inside the building, breathing fast and rubbing the sweat from his brow. "Hey …"

A look of relief flashed across Shianne's face. "Max, this is my husband, Gregory."

Gregory shook Max's hand.

"I was showing Shianne around again. I'd be happy to give you a tour of the place. We've remodeled the space quite a bit."

"I love the window space," Michelle observed. "It brings such depth and warmth inside. If I were a customer, I would love to eat here. Even with no furniture, it feels comfy."

Shianne nodded.

Max gestured toward Gregory. "The traffic flow is incredible. There's a large business park five minutes away. People can run in and get a bite to eat or pick up donuts on the run. You should do well here, Shianne, if your pastries are as great as you claim."

"Man, are you crazy?" Michelle interjected. "Everything Shianne cooks is good."

As the group took another tour of the building space, Shianne visualized where she would arrange everything.

"What do you think, Gregory? You haven't said anything," Shianne said.

He crossed his arms in front of his chest. "It's larger than what we discussed, which means the utility costs will be higher. And, more than likely, we'll have to increase our budget to buy more furniture and equipment. What do you think?"

"I like it. We won't have to do a lot of remodeling, and it has enough space for our customers and us. I love the office space in the rear. The advantages far outweigh the disadvantages." Shianne stood silent for a few moments. More than anything, she wanted Gregory's blessing, but she felt Grandma Eva's spirit rising in her saying, *Take it!*

She took a deep breath. "I'd love Scrumptious Bakery to open here, Gregory."

"Is this a yes?" Max asked.

Shianne looked into Gregory's eyes. Her heart raced.

Gregory stared, unblinking, and then nodded.

"Yes! Let's do it," Shianne said.

"Great!" Max said. "We'll make the changes you recommended today, and the place is yours for doughnuts, Shianne."

"That sounds great!"

She turned to Gregory. "Maybe we can open in a month or two?"

He nodded. "Congratulations. I have to get back to work. I'll see you tonight."

Shianne nodded. "Yes. We have to celebrate. Come to Michelle's. I've made dinner." She hugged him and whispered, "Thanks, honey."

"We're having Shianne's chicken kebabs tonight," Michelle said as he opened the door.

"I'll be there."

Michelle and Shianne waited for him to close the door and then jumped up and down with excitement.

"Hey! Hey! Hey! Shianne's getting a bakery," Michelle sang, hugging her. "I'm so happy for you."

"Finally! Thank you, Jesus."

Shianne's eyes brightened with an idea. "Let's check out the competition. Mama's Pastries is a few blocks over on Griffin Street." She grinned. "I'll buy."

Michelle chuckled. "Let's go. You know I don't turn down any free meals from you."

Minutes later, Shianne and Michelle entered Mama's Pastries. The bakery was full of people, some buying pastries, while others were eating at tables. Michelle spotted a couple leaving and quickly claimed the vacant table.

Shianne surveyed the bakery. "I like how it's decorated …the wood flooring, glass canisters for the brownies and cookies, the blackboards listing the bakery's menu and specials. Cute."

"It's nice if you're going for the old-fashion look and feel. I thought you envisioned a more contemporary setting, one with a little more pizzazz like its owner."

"Yes, that's what I'm thinking." Shianne continued inspecting the place. "This bakery is huge, much larger than mine."

"They've been in business for several years, Shianne. What do you expect? And, they didn't open here. They were in a small spot across town."

"They certainly have a customer base. We'll do great if we can get half the customers they have."

"You'll get more than half. People love good food, and this is a community that enjoys eating out." Michelle tapped the table lightly. "Girl, cut it out. Stop creating tensions for yourself. I want you to repeat after me. 'I can do all things through Christ Jesus, who strengthens me.'"

"I can do all things through Christ Jesus, who strengthens me."

"Amen!"

"Amen!"

Michelle flapped her hands and stood as if she were shaking off the negative thoughts. "Now that we've gotten that out the way, let's eat. I'll buy. I'm trying Mama's chicken salad. I want to see how it compares to yours because you're the chicken salad queen."

"I'll have the spinach and mushroom quiche."

"All righty," Michelle said and stepped away.

Shianne pulled her cell from her purse and messaged Chef Brown. *It's a go! Scrumptious Bakery is opening soon! Yes!*

Several moments later, Michelle returned with the food and placed it on the table.

"Looks good," Shianne said, resting her cell on the table. The girls blessed the food, and Michelle bit into her sandwich.

Shianne waited for her response. "And?"

"It's good, but not as tasty as yours, girlfriend." Michelle gave Shianne a high five. "Uh-oh, Mama's Pastries is in trouble."

Shianne tasted the quiche. "It's good, but the crust isn't crispy enough. It's also rubbery from too many eggs." She smiled. "What a relief."

"Go Scrumptious. Go Scrumptious," Michelle said, dancing in her seat. "Let's try some of their pastries."

Michelle returned to the counter where she bought brownies, slices of red velvet and carrot cake, and chocolate chip and peanut butter cookies.

Shianne took the brownies and cookies from her when she returned. "You bought all this?"

"Yes. We have to do our research. The more, the better"

Shianne dipped her fork into the carrot cake and hesitated as if in deep thought. "I have something to tell you, but I don't want you to say anything to Erica."

"What?" Michelle asked, biting into a brownie.

"I took out a loan for the bakery, and I didn't tell Gregory."

"You what? Why did you do that?"

"I borrowed the money in case Gregory said no."

"You planned to go against his will? Girl, Gregory will flip when he finds out what you've done!"

"He's not going to find out." Shianne laid her fork onto the plate. "He kept waffling, Michelle."

Michelle gave her a grim look. "How much did you borrow?"

"Thirty grand. I have some equipment from my catering business, but it's not what I need for a full-size bakery."

Michelle's eyebrows drew closely. "You borrowed thirty thousand dollars?"

Shianne shrugged. "This is the closest I've gotten to own a bakery. I want this bakery so bad I can taste it." She bit into a cookie.

"I understand what it's like wanting something so badly. But Gregory's your husband, your partner. You should be making decisions with him, especially decisions of this magnitude."

Shianne shook her head back and forth. "My husband was changing his mind all the time. 'Yes, we'll do it.' 'No, we better wait.'" She pouted.

"But—"

"But what?"

"Well, where does he think the start-up money is coming from?"

"Mom and Dad lent me ten grand, and Gregory and I planned to use some of our savings to fund the rest."

"Then, back to my original question. Why did you borrow thirty thousand? Gregory will think you've lost your mind."

Shianne nodded. "Pretty much." She crisscrossed her arms before her. "I borrowed the money in case of an emergency. Besides, he didn't tell me when he took money out of our savings account to buy the bar."

"You didn't know?"

"No! He just did it."

Michelle looked at Shianne cross-eyed. "Well, where did you think the money came from to buy the bar?"

"I thought his father was buying the bar, and that Gregory was just helping him run it. I didn't find out the bar was his until his mother gave me a bank statement that had gone to her house. Gregory had them going there. That was when we first got married, and he handled our finances." She smirked. "You know that's not happening anymore."

"But two wrongs don't make a right, my friend. You can't deal with situational ethics."

The remark took Shianne aback, but she knew Michelle was forthright. "I'll repay the loan as soon as I can."

Michelle shook her head. "I hope so."

"Who knows? I might not need all of the money."

Michelle sat quietly.

"It'll be all right. You'll see." Shianne picked up her fork and held it. "Will you help with publicity? I need a brilliant campaign to announce the grand opening. We can advertise the opening in local community calendars and with the chamber of commerce. We can also ask local businesses to display a flyer of our grand opening in their windows."

Michelle remained silent.

"Come on! I see that smile curling on your face," Shianne teased. "You know you enjoy doing things like this. I haven't done PR in a while."

After college graduation, Shianne had worked in public relations before moving to St. Louis, where she met Gregory.

"I'll stick with the menu Grandma Eva and I planned. We'll offer cupcakes, cakes and pies, croissants, and fresh bread. And then there are the cookies: chocolate chip, peanut butter, and sugar."

"What about savory pies? You make great lobster and crab pies."

"I was thinking about it. And Chef Brown makes a mean vegetable and broccoli cheese soup."

"Sounds great," Michelle said, resting her elbows on the table. "But what about your chicken salad? You can't leave it out."

"If I add chicken salad to the menu, will you help your friend with marketing?" she asked, giving a puppy-dog look. "I'll keep you in chicken salad forever," she said, grinning.

"So, we're bartering now?" Michelle asked, wide-eyed. "I'm supposed to work for food? You should be glad I love you. Of course, I will."

"Great!" Shianne checked her watch. "I have to pick up Ki." She gathered her purse.

"Wait a minute … I'm enjoying you and Ki, but you are going home tonight after your fabulous dinner, right?"

"Yes, we're going home. I shouldn't have left. I don't know what got into me. I acted like a madwoman. I did call Gregory last night and wish him a good night."

Michelle covered her mouth as not to show her grin. "Girly, you should have seen yourself flying down the stairs with that bag. Erica and I looked at each other like, 'What is going on up in here?' You guys were on ten!" She paused. "I get it, though. You felt as if your dream was falling apart again."

Shianne nodded. "Enough about our problems. What's going on with you and the mysterious Darius Mathews?"

Michelle pouted. "Nothing at all, unfortunately."

Darius was a 36-year-old Chicago engineer Michelle had met at a greeting card store. Michelle was browsing the store's inventory when Darius asked her opinion about a birthday card he was buying for a friend. Being the businesswoman she was, Michelle referred Darius to her card website. He later emailed her to thank her for the help, and things blossomed from there. She and Darius talked on the phone and had confirmed a few dates, but each time, either she or he postponed because of work. He canceled more than she.

"I hope we get together soon because I'm wondering if he's married or in a serious relationship."

Aromas from the Kitchen wafted through the house for more than an hour, making Michelle hungry. She shut off her computer and went upstairs. Erica was helping Shianne get things ready for dinner.

"Hey, I didn't hear you when you came in," Michelle said. "How was work?"

Erica put her hand on her hip. "Don't ask. I'm working with the hardest client ever. She's never satisfied. She wants hardwood flooring, arched ceilings, granite countertops, an island, a fireplace, and five bedrooms for two hundred thousand. She has me showing her homes out of her price range. The last house I showed her was three-fifty."

"Goodness. Why won't people just buy what they can afford?"

"Girl, tell me about it. Some people want a BMW on a scooter budget."

They laughed.

"I could tell you so many funny stories. Maybe I should write a book. I'd name it, Diary of a Crazed Real Estate Agent."

"Are we waiting for Gregory?" Michelle asked. "I'm starved. I couldn't concentrate on work with smelling what was cooking up here."

"No. Gregory's in the living room with Ki."

Michelle nudged Erica with her hip. "We're sending Shianne and Kaiya home tonight," she mumbled.

Erica tossed small tomatoes into the bowl. "Yes. Send Shianne home to her husband."

"Did I hear my name?" Shianne asked suspiciously.

"I was telling Erica how much fun we've had and how I'm missing you guys already."

Shianne eyed her. "We've only been here a day. We haven't been here long enough for you to miss us."

Erica grinned. "Girl, Michelle said she was sending you and Kaiya home tonight."

Michelle gasped. "Good friend, you are."

"Well, I'm telling the truth."

"So, she was talking about me behind my back?" Shianne asked.

"Yep."

"Well, we are going home."

Shianne washed and dried her hands. "I'll get Gregory and Ki so we can eat."

Michelle and Erica helped carry the food to the dining room.

Gregory and Kaiya entered the room moments later and sat at the table.

"Honey, would you bless the food?" Shianne asked. Gregory prayed, and they followed with a loud, "Amen." The group talked about everything from Erica's real estate woes to Michelle's new card line, to Jill Scott's upcoming concert as they ate.

"I love Jill Scott. Do you want to go, honey?" Shianne asked.

"Sure. Her concert in Milwaukee last year was awesome."

Erica sighed. "Aaron doesn't go to concerts. Will you be my date, Michelle?"

"Uh, yeah. I'll go with you. You get the tickets since you asked me."

A surprised look fell on Erica's face. "I walked right into that one!"

"That you did. But look at it this way; you'll have a lovely date alongside you."

Kaiya laughed. "You guys are funny."

"We do a lot of laughing. That's what good friends do, Ki," Shianne said.

"Are good friends sad together too? Last night, Aunt Michelle and Aunt Erica were sad with you."

Shianne's facial expression drooped. "Yes, good friends are sad together, and they sometimes cry together."

"Jocelyn and I are good friends. We cried when Muffin died," Kaiya said.

"Muffin?" Erica asked.

"Jocelyn's cat," Shianne replied.

"I'm sure she felt better, seeing you loved Muffin too," Erica said.

Kaiya smiled. "She did."

Michelle rested back in her chair full. "Great dinner, Shianne."

"Yes, great, baby." Gregory checked his watch. "It's almost seven."

Michelle and Erica stood, knowing Shianne and Gregory had matters to discuss. "Kaiya, will you help us carry the dishes into the kitchen?" Michelle asked.

"Okay, Aunt Michelle." She picked up her plate and carried it out of the room.

Gregory waited until the girls were out of earshot. "So, are you coming home tonight?"

"Yes, I'm coming home."

A relieved look crossed his face. "Shianne, you can't keep calling your girlfriends every time we disagree about something."

She rolled her eyes. "I do not call them every time we get into an argument, and you know I don't. So, you can stop saying this. I apologize for leaving, but you know how much I want this bakery. Your indecisiveness was driving me crazy."

"All I said was Kaiya needs you around a little longer to help her get dressed for school and do homework."

"I told you I would comb her hair, bathe, and lay out her school clothes every night. All you have to do is fix her breakfast. You can't do that?" Shianne sat for a few moments again, wondering about his unexplainable demeanor. "Is everything okay? Is something going on that you haven't told me?"

Gregory rested his elbows on the table and clenched his hands together. "I didn't want to bother you with this, but I've heard rumors there may be some layoffs at the company. But so far, no one is confirming anything. I don't want to open the bakery until I see how things pan out. We'll need my income until the bakery can sustain itself."

Shianne contemplated telling Gregory about the loan, but she was afraid since they had just reconciled. She didn't want to start another fight.

"I don't think we need to worry about money right now. Let's trust we'll be all right. We can't put our lives on hold based on speculation."

She stroked his hand. "Honey, I'm sorry to hear this, but we'll be okay. Let's step out in faith. You saw the place. It's in a great spot. We'll have more than enough patrons. I feel it in my gut." She squeezed his hand.

Michelle entered the room, catching the affection. "Get a room."

"We have several rooms at 1202 Wentworth," Gregory said.

Michelle grinned. "Then get going to 1202."

Gregory yelled, "Kaiya, it's time to go home! Get your stuff!"

"I'll get our things," Shianne said, standing from the table and walking away.

Michelle finished washing dishes then went upstairs to talk with Shianne. Michelle sat on the bed while Shianne put her things into her travel bag. "You guys good?"

"Yes, we're fine. It upset Gregory when both of you showed up."

"That goes without saying. I should have followed my first mind and came alone."

She sat beside Michelle. "I think he's worried about being laid off."

"His company's laying off workers?"

"There are rumors this could be happening."

"This explains his hesitancy, Shianne."

Shianne nodded. "I get it. But we can't live our lives based on speculation. The bakery will be fine."

Michelle gave a soft smile. "I know you'll do everything in your power to make it work. That's for sure."

Shianne wrapped her arm around Michelle. "I can always count on you. You're my ride or die. I knew there was a reason I let you be my friend in second grade."

Michelle laughed. "First, I'm not riding everywhere with you, nor am I dying for you. Second, I let you be my friend. Don't get it twisted."

Shianne had worn thick glasses in grammar school, and the boys would often tease her. They'd call her Four Eyes and repeatedly pulled her long ponytails. One day, she'd gotten so fed up with the name-calling that she punched one of the boys in the face. Embarrassed, the boy drew his fist, ready to lay into Shianne, but Michelle had stepped between them, and he hit her book. The three had to stay after school every day for two weeks as a punishment, and the girl's friendship grew afterward.

"I was so mad at you, Shianne because Daddy put me on punishment for a month."

"I'm sorry, but no one told you to get involved. You jumped in as if I couldn't handle myself."

"You couldn't."

"I was going to kick Marshal's butt."

Michelle looked at her side-eyed and laughed.

"Whatever," she said, grabbing her bag and heading toward the door.

Gregory, Kaiya, and Erica were in the family room watching TV when Shianne and Michelle came downstairs.

"I'm ready," Shianne said.

"Dinner was great, Shianne," Erica said. "You know I'm taking some leftovers home."

"Don't you always?" Michelle said, laughing.

The group said their goodnights, and Erica and Michelle plopped onto the couch afterward.

"Everything's good with them?" Erica asked.

Michelle mulled the question for a moment. "I believe so."

Erica turned to her. "You don't sound very convincing."

"Shianne thinks Gregory is worried about losing his job. Layoff rumors are circulating at his company."

Erica slumped deep into the couch. "Well, let's pray it doesn't happen. Now is not the time for him to be losing his job."

Shianne unpacked the bags and readied Kaiya for bed. The three settled in Kaiya's room, she and Shianne lying in bed as Gregory sat at the foot reading Kaiya's favorite story, *Miranda and Brother Wind*. When Gregory finished reading, Kaiya remained awake; Shianne had fallen asleep.

"Mommy's asleep, Daddy. Don't wake her up. Let her sleep with me tonight."

Gregory had been hoping he and Shianne would do more than sleep that night. He thought he'd wait until Kaiya went to sleep and then awaken Shianne. He kissed her on the cheek. "Okay, baby. You and Mommy get some sleep. I'll see you guys in the morning."

"Goodnight, Daddy."

Gregory was showering when Shianne joined him several moments later.

"Hey," she said, pulling back the shower curtain.

Gregory grinned. "Hey, sweetie. I thought you were sleeping." He took her hand and helped her into the shower.

"I needed a catnap. It's been a long day. But I'm fine now."

CHAPTER FOUR

Bakery

Shianne, Gregory, Chef Brown, and his nephew, Frederick, were encircled in prayer when Michelle and Erica drove up to Scrumptious Bakery, the car's horn beeping as if they were in a parade.

"Are you crazy?" Shianne asked, her voice raising an octave. "It's five in the morning. Shush!"

"We know what time it is," Michelle said, whisking her bangs out of her face and exiting her white BMW SUV. Michelle expected Shianne would be out-of-this-world thrilled about her bakery's first day. Michelle surveyed the pink banner hanging on the storefront advertising the grand opening.

"Shianne, you've talked about owning a bakery since we were kids, and now you want me to be quiet? We played bakery every time I came over or you wouldn't play with me. No, I won't."

Michelle returned to the car and grabbed a small megaphone. "Come one, come all! Scrumptious Bakery opens today! It's the new destination stop for the best-tasting desserts in downtown Evanston."

Shianne's eyes widened, surprised at the bullhorn announcement. She stood silent for a few moments, realizing what Michelle had said.

"You're right. I should be more excited. I've worked too hard to open this bakery." Shianne did a little dance moving her body side to side. Erica joined in with her.

"That's better," Michelle said, grinning.

"I'm so excited I could do a backflip," said Erica, who had been a cheerleader in college, where she had met Shianne. "You know I still got it."

"No, no, no. That's all right." Shianne took Erica's hand in hers. "We can use your skills helping our customers today."

Shianne faced Michelle. "We were praying when you guys drove up."

Michelle walked over to the group and took Erica's other hand. "Prayer is good."

"Father God, thank you for this day. I've wanted a bakery all my life, and to see my childhood dream come true is such a blessing. I'm so grateful. Thank you for the opportunity, Father God." She sniffled. "And thank you, Grandma Eva, for dreaming with me. I so wish you were here with me today. But I know you're here in spirit. And finally, a big thank you, Father God, for my husband and my wonderful group of friends who fanned my dream over the years. In Jesus' Name, Amen."

"Amen!" the group shouted.

Shianne wiped the tears from under her eyes and pulled a set of keys from her jacket.

"Wait a minute," Michelle said. "Erica and I have a gift for you." Michelle withdrew a small black velvet box from her pocket and handed it to Shianne.

Shianne looked at her wide-eyed. "What's this?"

"Open it and see," Erica said.

Shianne opened the box, revealing a gold necklace adorned with a cake-shaped charm reading, Scrumptious Bakery. "Ooh, I love it. It's adorable." She hugged the girls. "Thank you so much." Tears pooled in her eyes as she held up the necklace for everyone to see before letting Gregory put it on her. She pressed her hand against the chain. "I love you guys."

"We love you too," Michelle and Erica said together.

"Let's get this show on the road," Chef Brown, a stout man with salt and pepper hair, said. "All this crying is making me cry. We have a few hours before opening." He started counting down. "Ten, nine, eight ..."

The others joined in. "Seven, six, five, four, three, two, one!" Michelle and Erica jumped up and down as Shianne opened the door.

Gregory flicked on the lights, where a spacious entryway led to purple and black checkerboard flooring, silver tables paired with purple chairs, and shiny glass display cases around the counter.

Robin Lawford, a thin woman with beady blue eyes and heavy makeup who owned the nearby bookstore, was first in line when the bakery opened at 11 a.m.

"Mm, it smells delicious in here," she said of the sweet smell of chocolate meshing with the scent of fresh-baked bread and blueberry muffins. She flashed a coupon in her hand. "I believe I get a pie. Says here, you're giving free pies to the first twenty-five customers." She looked around the bakery. "Looks like I fit the bill!"

"What's your pleasure? Cherry, key lime, or apple?" Shianne asked with a generous smile.

Robin scanned the display of pies. "Everything looks so tasty." Her eyes crisscrossed the desserts for another moment before she pointed at a key lime pie. "I haven't had a good key lime pie in a while."

"Key lime it is," Shianne said to Frederick, who stood beside her at the counter.

"Good choice," he said, removing a pie from the shelf and putting it inside a pink and purple Scrumptious Bakery box.

Michelle approached Shianne with a large pair of pink scissors. A photographer followed behind her. "Shianne, this is Michael Scott, a photographer from *The Courier*."

Shianne shook his hand. "Thanks for covering our grand opening, Michael. We certainly could use the publicity."

"Nice meeting you, Mrs. White."

Shianne faced Michelle and smiled. "Make sure you send Michael off with a box of our goodies for the newsroom staff. We want them to become customers as well."

Michael grinned. "That's mighty nice of you, Mrs. White."

Michelle waved for Gregory, Chef Brown, and the others to join them while Shianne patted her hair, ensuring her curls were in place. As Gregory and the others circled her, Shianne urged Robin to take a picture with the group. She thought getting the local chamber of commerce's president in the photo would make a terrific statement.

"Welcome to Scrumptious Bakery, where every bite reminds you of Grandma," Shianne cried out excitedly as she and Gregory snipped the pink bow. "We're so excited to open today." She wiped a steady stream of tears from her cheek. "I owe my love of baking to my Grandma Eva, who taught my sisters and me how to bake." She gestured at a picture of Grandma Eva hanging on the wall. "At five and six years old, we were whipping up everything from chocolate chip and peanut butter cookies to peach cobblers and three-layer cakes. But as we got older, my sisters did more of the tasting, leaving me and my grandmother cooking and baking. I didn't mind, because I had Grandma to myself." Her lip quivered. "Grandma Eva was supposed to open the bakery with me but she died earlier this year, unfortunately."

The crowd gasped at the revelation.

Shianne collected herself and then shortened the speech she and Michelle had spent hours writing. She praised Gregory and the others, kissing and hugging them all, and then thanking everyone for attending the grand opening. "Enjoy your treats," she concluded.

The crowd applauded and returned to nibbling on the desserts while Shianne resumed her chat with Robin a few moments longer.

"I like what you did with the place." Robin gazed at a large pink and purple sign above the display case that read Everything Scrumptious. "There's no hint a men's clothing store was here."

"Thank you," Shianne said, scanning the room.

"Let me get out of your way, Shianne. It looks like you have a heap of customers. Have a wonderful opening."

"Thanks again for coming, Robin."

"You'll be seeing a lot of me."

Shianne stepped away and meandered throughout the bakery greeting customers one after another. Her eyes sparkled with each introduction.

Bone-tired, Gregory fell asleep as soon as he climbed into bed, while Shianne lay unable to sleep. Images of people sampling her bite-sized desserts, and Grandma Eva's to-die-for caramel pecan cheesecake slices permeated her mind.

You were supposed to be here with me, Grandma Eva. We were supposed to open the bakery together.

Shianne punched a pillow as tears fell from her almond-shaped eyes and streaked her face.

A loud snore escaped Gregory's mouth, distracting Shianne from her thoughts. She turned on her side and faced him before shifting the white linen from her body and slipping out of bed onto the lush carpet. Dressed in pink-and-white-striped pajamas, she sauntered down the long hallway to her office and plunked on a gold leather chair. She turned on the desktop computer and clicked on *The Courier's* website. Seconds later, a screen opened brandishing a picture of Scrumptious Bakery with a headline reading, *Scrumptious Bakery Delights Downtown Sweet Tooths.*

Oh my god, the front page! She grinned, knowing Michelle had something to do with the prominent placing. She'd created a huge media campaign for the bakery, incorporating social media, TV, radio, and newspapers. Shianne flushed with joy as she read the article.

Gregory entered the room, shirtless and wearing green cotton pajama pants. "What are you doing up, baby?" He rubbed his eyes. "It's after midnight. It'll be five o'clock in no time."

"I know, honey. But I couldn't sleep." She patted the armchair next to her, gesturing him to sit beside her. "Look what *The Courier* wrote about us." Her voice rose as he rested his body in the chair and crossed his legs at the ankles. "We made the front page!"

Gregory's eyes fixed on the screen. "This is great! Fantastic!" He swung toward her. "I wonder how many people were at the opening."

"Frederick said over two hundred people."

He nodded. "I bet some people were from other bakeries checking us out." He ran a hand through his black, wavy hair. "I'm sure they left thinking they'd better step up their game." He smiled and kissed her on the cheek. "I'm proud of you, baby."

"I'm proud of us both. We did this together."

"No, you should be proud of yourself. You kept pressing for the bakery. I wasn't always in line with you."

Shianne thought of the countless fights they'd had over the bakery. By right, she could have gone on a tirade of I told you so's, but she restrained. Her Scrumptious Bakery was open, and that's all that mattered.

Gregory took her hand and held it. "Come on. You need to get some sleep so that Scrumptious Bakery can make more great headlines."

The two milled down the hallway and got into bed. Gregory massaged her back until she fell asleep.

Shianne awakened four hours later. A shower and early morning prayer had her refreshed and ready to start her day. She kissed Gregory and Kaiya before heading to the bakery.

Smells of fresh bread wafted outside Scrumptious Bakery as Shianne opened the door. Inside, Frederick was putting loaves of bread on the displays.

"Ooh, it smells good in here," Shianne said, inhaling the aroma. "The bakery breathes scrumptiousness. You guys beat me here."

"We've been here for about an hour. You know what they say, 'Early to bed, early to rise to make the cupcakes.'"

Shianne laughed. "Who says that? That's so corny."

Frederick laughed along with her.

"Thanks for a laugh anyway," she said.

Though Shianne had known Frederick for only a matter of weeks, he was growing on her. Frederick had a great personality and was a hard worker. He had lived in New York with Chef Brown, who had taken his nephew under his wings after a few incidents with police. Chef Brown had asked Shianne if she could use another set of hands when the bakery opened, and she welcomed the help.

"We made the front page in the paper today," Shianne said.

"I saw it on the internet," Frederick said excitedly.

"I'll buy a nice frame for the article and hang it in the store."

Customers ventured into the bakery throughout the day, keeping Shianne, Chef Brown, and Frederick on their feet most of the day. Shianne recognized some customers from the grand opening and was so pleased with their returning that she placed an extra tart or cream puff inside their bags.

CHAPTER FIVE

Michelle was on her way home from the post office when her cell buzzed. She glanced at the monitor in her car, and it read, Darius M. Her eyes widened. *Hmm, Mr. Mathews. What a pleasant surprise.* She answered.

"Hi, pretty lady," he said, his voice rich and sonorous.

Michelle pretended not to recognize the voice. "Darius?"

"Yes, this is him. How are you?"

"I'm great, and you?"

"Fantastic! I'm on my way back to the city, and I wondered if you'd like to meet for coffee or dinner?"

Michelle eyed her ripped jeans and grimaced. She wished she was wearing something more pleasing, like her Apple Bottom jeans and a cuter top. But, eager to see him again, she accepted and suggested a restaurant.

Driving into the restaurant's parking lot, Michelle saw a few empty spots near the entrance but parked elsewhere. She didn't want Darius to see her primping. Combing through her short bob hairdo, Michelle frowned at missing yesterday's hair appointment. She needed a perm; the lines around her hairline were more curly than straight. She then applied fresh makeup to her pecan brown skin and peppered her body with perfume before exiting the car.

A tall, handsome man with Milk Dud-colored skin and deep-set brown eyes stood in the doorway. Michelle's mouth opened. Her eyes lit up. Heat radiated through her chest. *Hallelujah! I don't remember him being this handsome.* Darius stood about six feet tall, with a muscular build and a contagious smile.

"Hello, Michelle."

She smiled. "Hey, Darius."

He embraced her. "You're prettier than I remember."

"Thank you." Her eyes expressed delight.

Within moments, a hostess greeted them and led them to a table. They stared at each other for a few moments before Darius opened the conversation. "I'm glad we're getting together. I was at a meeting in Milwaukee most of the day and thought I'd reach out to you on my way home."

"It was nice hearing from you. I was running errands when you called."

A waitress set two glasses of water before them. "Hello, my name is Myra, and I'll be your waitress tonight. Are we ready to order?"

Darius glanced at the waitress. "Would you give us a few moments, please?"

"Sure," she said and walked away.

"I hope you're not in a hurry to order," he said, holding a menu. "I'm excited to see you, and I don't want to rush through dinner."

Michelle blushed. "Are you kidding? I'm famished." She shook her head, eyes gleaming mischievously. "Just kidding."

Darius flashed a smile, and with a curious look on his face, said, "I don't want to make you feel uneasy, but can I ask you something?"

"Sure."

"When we talked earlier, you mentioned you were on a dating site. What's a beautiful woman like you doing on a dating site?"

Beautiful women are looking for love too. Just because you're pretty doesn't mean men are knocking down your door. Well, the right men. Michelle gave a confident grin. "I could ask you a similar question. You're a handsome man. Why are you on a dating site? One would think you could date any woman you choose."

A surprised look flashed across his face at the cheeky response. "Okay, you got me. But, if you must know, I joined the site after you said you were on it. I was hoping to learn more about you."

"Really? No way. You know people lie on those sites."

"Yes, way." Darius toyed with his napkin. "The picture you've posted doesn't do you justice." His grin forced the dimple under his eye to twinkle. "You're gorgeous."

Michelle blushed. "Aw, you're sweet."

He leaned back against the booth with a checkmate look on his face. "Now, your turn."

"Well, my friend Erica is always suggesting I try online dating. She met a nice guy on the site and thought I might do the same."

"Have you?"

"I've met a few guys who have gotten my attention, but..."

A crease wrinkled his forehead. "But what?"

Michelle shrugged. "Nothing materialized."

The two sat quietly until Darius broke the silence again.

"I came across your cards at a store in the city last week. You should be proud of yourself."

Michelle grinned, flattered by the compliment. "So, did you buy any?"

"I did. I bought two in fact—one for my mother and sister. They loved them. I told them I knew the woman who owned the card company. Both of them said they would shop for your cards the next time they need one. So I guess you have a few more fans."

Michelle's grin stretched from ear to ear. "Thank you, and tell them thanks for the support. Which cards did you buy?"

"My sister recently participated in a 5K marathon, but she didn't finish because her leg cramped after two miles. So, I got her the card saying, 'You're my horse, even if you never win a race.'"

Michelle smiled. "Ah, I love that saying. I get a lot of my expressions from my Aunt Vi, whose now deceased. She had a canny way of phrasing things."

He raised an eyebrow and leaned forward. "I'm sorry."

"Thank you. Aunt Vi was so clever. And, she was funny as heck. I loved listening to her, especially after I started designing cards. Many of her sayings were original, but some she said came from growing up in the South."

"It sounds like Aunt Vi was quite an inspiration to you."

"She was. I miss her so much. We had a good time whenever we were together. We'd laugh ourselves silly."

Darius sipped from his glass of water. "We never talked about how you got started making cards."

She grinned. "Well, I started in college. I was falling in love with this guy but I didn't know how to tell him. So, I thought I'd buy a card to express my feelings. However, I couldn't find a card that said exactly what I was feeling," she said, shaking her head. "I searched every store in town that I thought sold greeting cards. So, unable to find one, I decided to make my own card. My boyfriend loved it, and so had my friends, who then asked me to make cards for them."

He smiled. "So you made lemonade from lemons, huh?"

"She brandished a wide smile. Yes. I never thought I'd make a career out of this. I've had my greeting card business for two years. I'd worked in marketing for several years prior."

"What a great story," Darius said. He picked up his glass of water and took a sip. "So, tell me, what are you looking for in a man?" he asked with piercing eyes.

"Ah, the fifty thousand-dollar question." She hesitated, and then looked deeply into his eyes. "I'm looking for a man who smiles with his eyes when he looks at me, a man who I can read his thoughts by his touch, and hear the love he has for me in his laughter."

Darius swallowed. "People often talk about loyalty and honesty when discussing what they want in a mate."

"I want that too but . . ."

Michelle shifted in her seat. "What about you, Darius? What are you looking for in a woman?"

"Well, trust and honesty are big for me. I want a woman who I can trust. I've been in far too many untrusting relationships." He glanced up for a moment. "I also want her to be sweet, classy, and sassy."

"Classy and sassy?" Michelle opened her hands for him to expound on his answer.

"Yes. While classy, I want my woman to be a little feisty, have a little edge. I want her to be bold and lively."

Michelle wondered if she fit the description.

"Besides these things, I want a woman who can make me feel invincible, a woman who can touch my soul. Is this you, Michelle?"

Michelle felt her body warming. She wanted to say, *Yes, that's me*, but instead said, "That's a question you'll have to answer."

Darius raised an eyebrow. "I believe you can answer it."

Michelle gave him a curious eye as the waitress returned to the table to take their orders.

Michelle and Darius spent the rest of the evening, chatting as if they had known each other for years. Michelle noticed that the more Darius spoke, the more his good looks took second place to his charming personality. She loved that they could talk about anything—politics, food, travel.

Michelle loved listening to him talk about his siblings. Being an only child, Erica and Shianne was the closest to a sister she had. "You're lucky you had your brothers to play with. I'm an only child. I had my cousin, Paul, who I hung around a lot. But I wanted sisters."

"Sometimes my brothers had me wishing I had no siblings," Darius said, chuckling.

"I had two imaginary sisters, Tasha and Chloe."

He laughed.

She leaned in and whispered, "We talked about everything—boys, school, even about my parents. We'd even fight!"

"Fight?" He snickered and stared at her side-eyed. "Uh-oh, you aren't getting weird on me, are you?"

"No. Not at all."

"So, when you're with your real friends, what do you like to do?"

"My girlfriends, Shianne and Erica and I do a lot of shopping, or we just hang out at each other's homes." She removed her cell phone from her purse and showed him a picture of the three.

"Wow, you're all beautiful. I bet you ladies get a lot of play from the men."

"We do—did. Shianne's married now. We don't hang out as much as we used to because of family and work, but we talk every day. Shianne opened a bakery recently, so she spends a lot of her time there.

"What do you like to do, Darius?"

"I love camping and taking long drives. I'll get in my car and drive for hours."

"I love road trips," Michelle said excitedly. "The next time you go on one of those long drives, call me. I might go with you."

"I definitely will." He winked. "Is there anywhere, in particular, you'd like to go?"

"I'd love to drive to Canada."

"I've been to Canada several times—Toronto, Niagara Falls, and Quebec City. It's a beautiful country. You'd enjoy it."

They both smiled at the thought of having something in common.

Darius cleared his throat. "While it's not in Toronto, would you like to go to my friend's art show this weekend?"

Michelle thought for a moment. "Sounds like a lot of fun. Who's your friend?"

"Monroe Therman."

Michelle put her palm to her chin. "No, I haven't heard of him, but certainly, I'd like to go."

"I believe you'll like his work. He's a talented artist. The showing is at the Stony Island Arts Bank in Chicago. You can bring your friends if you'd like."

"I'll ask Erica to come along. Can we meet you there?"

"Well, I was hoping to pick you up, but … sure."

Darius gave her the details as they finished eating. "I'm glad we got together. I had fun."

"I enjoyed your company," she said, saddened at their dinner ending. "It was nice seeing you again."

After paying for their meals, Darius walked Michelle to her car. "I'm looking forward to Saturday," he said, opening her car door.

"So am I. Goodnight."

Darius closed the door after she slid in and tapped the hood of the car. Michelle drove away with a big smile on her face. She was so excited about meeting Darius that she called Shianne to tell her they'd gotten together.

"I bet you can't guess where I've been and who I've been with."

"I don't know, but, by the sound of your voice, it was someplace fun and with someone special."

"I had dinner with Darius."

"Darius? Well, it's about time! I bet you're shining like a pair of red rubber boots."

Michelle laughed and looked at herself in the rearview mirror. She was glowing. "I was coming home from the post office when he called and asked if I could meet him for dinner. Girl, I have on my worst pair of ripped jeans, and a red sweater. I started to say no but met him anyhow—ugly jeans and all."

"Knowing you, you were ugly jeans chic."

Michelle grinned. "Of all days, I'm wearing tennis shoes and not my cute little pumps." She sighed. "That's okay, though. We had a good time. Darius is fascinating and so funny."

"Those are nice qualities to have."

"We were at the restaurant for over two hours. I think I like him."

"It sounds like you do."

Michelle slapped the steering wheel. "Girl, Darius is TGOF."

"A tall glass of fine," Shianne said, chuckling.

"He didn't look this handsome the first time we met. I don't know what I was thinking. I never overlook a fine man."

"So, when will you see him again?"

"We're getting together Saturday. He invited me to his friend's art show in the city."

"That sounds like fun."

"I'm thinking about asking Erica to come with if she isn't busy." Michelle smiled. "I'll dress up this time. He complimented me on my looks with the jeans. Imagine what he'll say when he sees me all dolled up. I think I'll give him a little leg action."

"Oh no, not the legs!"

"Yes, time to show him the shapely. Hmm, maybe I'll buy a new outfit."

"You have plenty of clothes to wear. Go to the Michelle closet. I'm sure you'll find something in there."

"I'm going to splurge, girl. I haven't bought anything new for myself in months."

Michelle and Shianne chitchatted until she reached home. While getting ready for bed, her phone alerted her she had a text. She clicked the message that opened to a large bouquet of red roses. Her heart fluttered. Underneath the flowers, Darius had typed, *I can't stop thinking about you.*

Michelle grinned and reread the message. *You have me smiling*, she texted back.

That's my intent.

See you on Saturday.

Yes! Saturday. Goodnight.

Michelle sat for a few moments, adoring the bouquet and wondering if Darius would be her new guy. She then texted Erica and invited her to lunch the next day. I *hope you're ready for some fun,* her text concluded. She believed Erica would read between the lines and figure out her message.

CHAPTER SIX

Michelle had a blast shopping the next day. She sang lines from James Brown's "I Feel Good" as she went from store to store. By the time she had met up with Erica, she had bought two outfits, three pairs of shoes, jewelry, and perfume.

Erica sashayed into the restaurant, beautiful as ever, wearing designer sunglasses, a navy-blue pinstripe suit, and matching three-inch heels. Bronze coloring highlighted her curled hair. "Hey, girl," she said, hugging Michelle and eyeing the bags beside her. "It looks like you bought a few things." Erica slid into the booth seat across from her.

"Macy's had a great shoe sale."

"Ooh, do I see a pair of Christians in the bag?"

"Indeed, you do. I treated myself today, girl." Michelle pulled one of the purple pumps from the bag and handed it to Erica.

"I like these," she said, eyeing the shoe and its red bottoms before handing it back to Michelle. "You indulged yourself well."

A waiter brought two glasses of water to the table.

"Could we have some lemon wedges, please?" Michelle asked.

"Sure," he said and walked away.

"Do you have any plans for the weekend?" Michelle asked.

"No. Aaron is going out of town, so I'm free," Erica said with a hint of satisfaction. "He's driving to Minnesota with his cousin to visit his aunt. What are you doing this weekend?"

"Darius invited me to his friend's art show."

"Darius? So this is what the urgent luncheon text was about last night." She smiled.

"Want to come with?"

"Sure, I'd like to go. I haven't been to an art show in a while. I'd also like to meet this new man of yours."

"He's not my man, at least not yet."

They both grinned.

"I believe you'll like Darius," Michelle said. "We should have fun."

Erica hadn't liked Michelle's last few boyfriends. She disliked Curtis, a mechanic, who Michelle had met at a car wash. He didn't fit the mold of most of the men she had dated—tall, dark, handsome, and conversational. Curtis was thin and maybe a half-inch shorter than Michelle's five-foot-eight frame. But Curtis was smart and could take a car apart without looking. They dated for a few months before the relationship tanked.

And Erica hated Brandon, the boyfriend before that, to the core. She had no tact when it came to him. She told him off in a grocery store one day after Michelle's split with him. He'd cheated on Michelle.

"We both know you have a potty mouth that can spill those expletive deletes like crazy, but please refrain from them, okay?"

Erica gave her an odd look. "What are you talking about?"

She mulled for a few moments. "Oh, Brandon. Are you still mad at me for telling him off? I thought you were over that."

"This has nothing to do with Brandon. It's about tact or your lack of it. Can you be nice even if you don't like him?"

"I'm always nice to your male friends. I don't know how you can say I'm not."

"You cursed Brandon out in the middle of a grocery store, Erica.

One of my mother's church members was in the store and heard you. Our business got back to my mother. Do you know how embarrassing that was for me? Mama was talking about barring you from her house!"

Erica's eyelashes fluttered. "I just told him to take his lame-ass back to Minnesota because you didn't want him. Yes, I cussed him out. He needed it. Again, I'm sorry it got back to your mother, but, girl, I was furious!" She took a drink of water. "Mama Anthony loves me. She would never ban me from her house."

Michelle shook her head. She knew Erica was right. Though her mother felt Erica was over the top, she loved both Erica and Shianne dearly. Michelle recalled the horrible scene where she had caught Brandon with another woman. "I guess you were right. You should have sucker-punched him!"

A smirk crept on Erica's face. "See, I was justified at lashing out at him." She heaved her hand in the air. "Enough of that bad dream. We'll have so much fun this weekend." She rocked in her seat to background music playing in the restaurant. "Big fun!"

Erica arrived at Michelle's a half-hour early wearing a tight Michael Kors black dress. "I know I'm early, but I came straight from work." She removed her black-and-white checked coat and plunked down on Michelle's bed.

"That's okay," Michelle said as she applied makeup to her face. "Is that how you go to work, girl?" she asked, scanning Erica's outfit. "Nice."

"Thank you. And your leather skirt is showing off the curvy quite well. Are you wearing your new purple heels? They'll look great with it." Erica stood from the bed and moseyed to the mirror alongside Michelle. "New lipstick?"

Michelle nodded and continued applying the purple matte lipstick.

"That color looks great on you. So does that nail polish." Michelle stuck out her hands to give Erica a full view of her berry-hued fingernails.

Erica raised her head and sniffed the air. "And you're wearing a new perfume? Are all these changes to go to an art show, or are you trying to impress Darius?"

Michelle turned from the mirror and studied Erica. "I change my lipstick and perfume all the time, and you know it." She smiled. "I am excited, though."

"I know you are. I haven't seen you this enthusiastic about a date in a while. Good for you."

Michelle ran her fingers through her hair. "I don't know how long we'll be hanging out tonight. I have so much work to do."

"Girl, you can do that tomorrow. You work all the time. You need to get out and have some fun, let your hair hit the floor. Twirl a little."

"My work is fun."

"But it's lonely fun." Erica brought her index finger to her mocha-colored skin. "Let me see. There's you, you, and you who make the cards. I bet you guys have a great time together."

Michelle grinned. "Stop it. And, you're one to talk. We hardly see you anymore. You're always working or hanging out with Aaron."

Erica made a dismissive noise. "So, tell me more about this Darius guy."

"I've told you what I know about him. You can play twenty questions with him later."

Darius stood outside the Stony Island Arts Bank when Michelle and Erica drove up. His tall stature was the first thing Michelle noticed outside the gray terra cotta building. The Stony Island Arts Bank had been a vibrant community saving and loan in Chicago's South Shore neighborhood in the early 1900s but had closed in the 1980s. The building had remained vacant for decades until artist Theaster Gates purchased it for one dollar and converted it into an African-American cultural center and gallery.

Darius smiled as Michelle and Erica approached him. "You look beautiful."

"Thank you. Darius, this is my friend Erica James. Erica, Darius Matthews."

Erica smiled. "I know, Darius."

"Hey," he said. "How are you?"

"I'm doing fine. How about you?"

"Great!"

Michelle looked at them with a puzzled expression. "So, you know each other?"

They both nodded.

"What a small world," Michelle said.

Erica glimpsed at a couple entering the building. "I'm going inside, okay? I saw some friends I'd like to say hi to."

Michelle nodded and faced Darius. "So you know Erica? How do you know her?"

"We met some months ago. I dated a coworker of hers." His comment took Michelle aback. She quickly thought of who Darius could have dated. She had met most of Erica's coworkers at office events, and most were married, except Renee and Carolyn. Curious, she asked, "Care to tell me who?"

"I dated Carolyn Brewer for a few months."

Michelle tried avoiding his eyes. "Carolyn?"

"Yes. Are you ready to go inside?" Darius asked, avoiding further comment. "I don't want Monroe thinking I ran out on him."

"Sure."

Darius took her hand and led her into the gallery. A crowd circled Monroe, who was talking about his paintings. Michelle tried giving Monroe her full attention but couldn't. Her thoughts kept traveling back to Carolyn. Carolyn was a sweet girl, Michelle thought, but Erica had referred to her as CC—or Crazy Carolyn, in some of their discussions. At the time, Michelle paid no attention, but now that she had learned Carolyn and Darius had dated, she wanted to know more about CC.

Michelle wondered whether she should quiz him more about Carolyn or wait until another time. She decided on the latter, thinking she could get more information from Erica later.

Following Monroe's discussion, Darius and Michelle meandered hand in hand through the center, laughing and talking while viewing his art. Monroe was an impressive artist, Michelle thought, and by the end of the night, she and Erica had bought a painting.

"I hope you enjoyed tonight," Darius said, loading the portraits into her car as she got inside.

"I did. I had a great time."

He bent down and kissed her on the cheek. "I'll call you tomorrow, okay? Goodnight, Erica."

Erica waved goodbye, and Michelle started the engine and drove off.

"Unbelievable!" Erica said. "I never would have guessed he was the Darius you were talking about. Whoa!"

"This is so weird. Did Darius and Caroline date for a long time?"

"He told you about her? I'm liking him more already."

Michelle nodded. "Yes. Why wouldn't he?"

"They didn't date very long. I believe they met at a friend's wedding. Carolyn was goo goo ga ga over him. She was always talking about him—Darius this, Darius that."

"That's understandable. Darius is charming. You can say what you want about Carolyn, but she has excellent taste in men. At least in Darius."

"Carolyn accused him of cheating, but I don't know. She fudges the truth sometimes. She's also spoiled, and when she doesn't get her way, she throws a fit. Maybe he didn't want to put up with that. It was a big surprise to everyone when they broke up." Erica grinned. "Well, he's interested in you now, so have fun. He seems like a nice guy."

Erica touched Michelle's coat sleeve. "You guys looked like you were thoroughly enjoying each other. Did you have fun? I saw how he was looking at you all sappy, patting you on the shoulder, and holding your hand as you went through the gallery. And you had the biggest grin on your face. You were smiling like Chester the Cheetah."

"I was not."

"Yes, you were. Wait 'til I tell Shianne."

Michelle burst out laughing. "Cut it out. Was I that obvious?"

Erica nodded. "Girl, your face was lit up like Christmas tree lights."

The two laughed heartily.

"Well, we'll see if anything comes of this," Michelle said.

Michelle was hopeful Darius would become her boyfriend and not just someone she dated a few times. She adored him. It was unusual for her to have such feelings for a guy so early in a relationship.

CHAPTER SEVEN

Bakery

Butterflies fluttered in Michelle's belly all day. Thoughts of seeing Darius again made her nervous. She'd tidied her home and cleaned the kitchen twice, although it wasn't needed. Michelle didn't cook much, and her dirty dishes often amounted to a few glasses and saucers. She wanted her kitchen sparkling clean since Darius would be cooking. She'd set the table with a flower centerpiece and her best dishes.

Darius arrived at six that evening with his trademark grin and three grocery bags. He followed Michelle to the kitchen, gazing at the house décor as he went. He laid the bags on the black and white marble countertop and removed his coat, revealing a navy blue sweater and matching corduroy slacks.

"You look nice," Michelle said. "Let me take your coat?"

"Thank you," he said, handing her his jacket.

The sweet scent from his coat was enchanting. *Sexy*, Michelle thought as the smell of musk cologne filled her senses.

"I like your place."

"Thank you."

Michelle had made few changes in the months she'd been there. She loved Aunt Vi's eclectic style and didn't want to change things.

Darius withdrew a bag of rice, French bread, a bottle of wine, and a large green covered bowl from the bags.

She patted the bowl. "I hope this is what I think it is." During earlier telephone conversations, Darius and Michelle both had admitted their love for gumbo.

He grinned. "Take a look."

Michelle uncovered the bowl of shrimp, sausage, crab, peppers, onions, and celery swimming in a thick, dark roux. "Yes! Gumbo!" She wanted to jump up and down, but she shot Darius a wide smile instead. "Thanks for sharing. I love me some gumbo."

"I had it in the freezer, so I thought I'd bring it for dinner." He looked at her adoringly. "I'll bring it over every time if I get to see that beautiful smile of yours."

Michelle blushed.

"Okay, let's get started." He scanned the light-colored kitchen with matching glass door cabinets and steel appliances. "I'll need two pots, one for the gumbo and one for the rice."

Michelle owned every kind of pot and pan thanks to Aunt Vi, unlike her apartment, where she'd owned one skillet and one large pot.

Once the rice was boiling and the bread was in the oven, Darius opened the wine.

Michelle retrieved two burgundy wine glasses from the cabinet.

"What should we toast to?" Darius asked as he poured wine into the glasses.

"Let's toast to friendship."

Darius raised his glass. "To friendship." They clinked glasses and sipped.

"Mm, this is nice," Michelle said.

"It's a Chianti. It's my favorite wine."

Michelle set her glass on the counter and walked toward the sound system. "What kind of music do you like?"

"I love old school. I was listening to Earth, Wind & Fire driving here. Do you have any of their music?"

"Are you serious? I have a lot of their music." She inserted a CD into the player and one of the group's most well-known songs, "Keep Your Head to the Sky," played. She overheard Darius singing along when she returned.

"You have a nice voice."

He smiled. "Thank you. I sang in a band in my late teens."

"I bet that was fun. What happened to the group?"

"We went our separate ways when we went to college. I still sing publicly on occasion. I also play drums."

"Umm, you're an engineer and a musician. Well, the next time you're performing, let me know. I'd love to come and hear you."

He took another sip of wine. "Sure. I definitely will."

Gumbo perfumed the kitchen as they chatted. Darius amused Michelle with his stories. One, in particular, was about the first time he'd cooked for a woman. The dinner was lasagna, garlic bread, and salad. "I was working it," he said, placing the gumbo on the table and taking a seat. "I had followed my sister's directions to a T. I even added extra cheese."

"So, I take it all went well?" Michelle asked with a raised eyebrow.

Darius spooned gumbo into their bowls. "It was disastrous. I forgot to boil the noodles."

"Oh, no! You forgot to boil the noodles?" She shook her head. "Let us pray." Michelle grinned and bowed her head.

Darius prayed over the food, and Michelle responded with a loud, "Amen!"

"How could you forget to boil the noodles?"

"I guess I was so nervous that I forgot. Maybe I thought the noodles would cook in the oven. I should have bought the noodles that didn't require boiling."

"Crunch. Crunch," she said, laughing. "So, what did you do?"

"I threw it away and took her out to dinner."

"This is hilarious. I bet you thought you were the man until you bit into it."

He picked up his fork. "Yes, I was feeling good. I was the man." He rested back in the chair. "I bet you've messed up a meal or two for a guy."

Michelle shook her head. "No. I can't say I have."

"Come on, Michelle. You know you have."

"No, I haven't."

Michelle straightened. "Now, I have made a few mistakes but none had to do with food."

Darius looked at her intently.

She recalled the time she'd tried putting oil in a date's car. He had run into the gas station to buy a second quart of oil, and while away, Michelle decided to pour in the first quart without him. She had seen her father put oil in his car several times, so she thought it was a no brainer. But, instead of pouring oil into the oil tank, she poured it into the antifreeze reservoir.

"You did what? That's horrifying." Darius shook his head in disbelief.

"It was ghastly."

"Was the car damaged?"

"Luckily for me, an auto repair shop was next door. They cleaned the reservoir with a degreaser and refilled the coolant. This happened years ago." She laughed. "The guy and I are still friends today. We laugh about it every time we talk."

"Now, that's funny."

He glanced at Michelle's plate. "Looks like you're enjoying the gumbo. Is it cooked well enough for you?"

She smiled. "Yes. It's delicious."

After dinner, they watched a movie and cuddled. Darius left late in the evening.

"Next time, I want you to cook for me," he said, putting on his jacket, and then kissing her on the cheek.

Michelle smiled, excited he wanted another date. "I'd love to. What would you like me to cook for you?"

"I'm serious."

"So am I."

"Surprise me," he said, walking to the door.

Michelle followed and stood in the doorway as he left his fragrance lingering behind. *Darius Mathews, you have fantastic swag,* she thought, watching him walk to his car.

Michelle was drifting off to sleep when her phone chimed alerting her of a message. She grabbed the phone from the nightstand and clicked on the text. It was from Darius.

We forgot to hang your picture! it read, followed by a smiling face emoji.

We did! Hopefully, you can hang it soon, she responded, adding a smiling emoji.

Would you like to go to a movie this weekend?

Yes, I'd like that.

Darius sent her a promo for the movie *If Beale Street Could Talk* and wrote *Saturday?*

Yes. Saturday is fine.

I'll give you a call.

I'm looking forward to us getting together again. Good night.

Michelle turned off the cell and placed it back on the nightstand. She lay in bed, covers pulled to her neck, thinking of Darius until she fell asleep.

CHAPTER EIGHT

Bakery

Things were going well for the White family. Scrumptious Bakery was establishing itself as a fantastic downtown Evanston bakery, and things were great at home. It was a Wednesday morning, and Gregory had made breakfast for Kaiya before dropping her off at school. After arriving to work, his secretary handed him his messages; one was from his boss, who wanted to meet with him first thing.

"Do you know if Bob will be at the meeting, Felicia?"

Bob was another assistant manager at Triax Corporation, a custom software company.

"I don't know," Felicia responded.

Gregory grabbed a notepad from his desk and headed to his boss's office. As the elevator climbed to the second floor, he wondered what the meeting was concerning. His boss hadn't mentioned it to him at closing yesterday when they walked out of the building together. They'd chatted about golf.

"Good morning, Tammy," Gregory said.

She smiled. "Good morning. Tom is waiting for you." Tammy buzzed her boss, notifying him that Gregory was there.

Tom gave a nervous smile as Gregory entered the room, and sat in the brown leather chair in front of his desk.

Tom crossed his hands in front of him and said, "I don't know how to say it, Greg, but the company is laying you off."

Gregory gave a surprised look. He wondered if he'd heard Tom correctly. "Did you say laid off?"

Tom nodded and snatched a paperclip from his desk. "I fought hard to keep you, but I couldn't change any minds," he said, toying with the clip.

Gregory's heart pounded. He felt as if he couldn't breathe as he scooted to the edge of the chair. "Laid off? Why, Tom?"

"You and I have been talking about this for a while. We knew this was a possibility. I honestly didn't think you would be one of those to go."

Gregory stood and paced back and forth. "I brought money into this company. I worked my ass off for this company. I thought we were on the upswing!"

"No one can disagree with you on this. I'm just as shocked as you."

The room quieted for a moment before Tom continued. "You'll receive a severance package."

Gregory approached Tom's desk and leaned in close to him. "Did Bob get laid off too?"

Tom shook his head, continuing to play with the paperclip. Gregory's jaw tightened. "That's interesting because I trained Bob!"

"I can't explain the reasoning behind keeping him, Greg. Maybe they kept him because he's making less money than you. I don't know."

"Did you lose your job, Tom?"

Tom's gaze darted away from Gregory. A lump formed in his throat. "No."

Gregory didn't want to play the race card with him, but the thought was crossing his mind. "I hope race has nothing to do with this."

Tom looked up, red-faced. "Come on, Greg. Let's not go there, at least not with me."

"Well, what am I supposed to think?" Gregory felt terrible for the comment, knowing Tom had been a great friend. It was he who had recommended Gregory's job transfer to Chicago.

"I don't know what the future holds for any of us here. I could be out next week."

Gregory rubbed his hands together. "So, when am I out?"

"In two weeks."

"Two weeks?" Gregory frowned as he slid into the chair. He felt sick to his stomach.

"Don't make me out to be the bad guy, Greg."

Gregory glared at Tom. "I'm not, but I wish I hadn't transferred. I wouldn't be making as much money, but I would still have a job."

Tom's eyes narrowed.

Gregory stormed from the office, his heart beating as if his chest would explode. When he reached his office, he slammed the door behind him.

Felicia tapped lightly on the door moments later. Gregory collected himself and sought to look brave.

"Come in."

Felicia peeked inside before entering. Gregory stood, staring out the window as Felicia opened the door more fully.

"Is everything all right? You looked upset when you returned from your meeting."

Gregory sighed sadly. "I was let go, Felicia."

"They fired you?"

"They laid me off, but same difference. I don't have a job."

Felicia covered her mouth with her hand. "Why? How could they do this to you? You're the best assistant manager here. This is ridiculous!" She leaned back against the wall and sighed.

The two looked at each other for a moment before she said, "So, I guess I'm next."

"Tom didn't say anything about your position, so I guess you still have a job. When I meet with HR, I'll recommend they keep you, although I don't know if they'll listen to me."

Gregory walked over to his desk and sat. "Have you seen Bob?"

"Pamela said he called in sick."

"Yeah, he's sick, all right. I bet he knew they were laying me off today."

"Bob didn't lose his job? That's interesting. Everyone in the company knows he's a poor manager, that he does just enough to get by."

"Well, mediocre or not, he still has a job." Gregory grabbed his jacket and briefcase and strode toward the door. "I'll see you tomorrow, I guess. I don't want to give this place any more of my time. I don't want to answer another telephone call, talk to another customer."

"I understand." Felicia watched as he trudged to the elevator.

Tears filled Gregory's eyes as he drove to a nearby park. He felt powerless and distraught. All he could think of was how he would tell Shianne about his job loss. *I don't understand this. A few hours ago, I was so happy with how things were going with the family. Now, I feel like a train wreck.*

Gregory focused on a young boy and girl racing toward a slide, their voices excited as their mother followed behind. *Better have fun while you can kids because life is a beast. It will spin you upside down when you least expect it.*

Gregory slumped into his seat and rehearsed what he would say to Shianne for more than an hour before driving to the bakery.

It was lunchtime, and Shianne and Frederick were waiting on customers when Gregory strode into the bakery.

"Hey, honey," Shianne said. "You look tired. Are you feeling all right?"

"We need to talk." Gregory went through the kitchen, passing Chef Brown as if he hadn't noticed him.

"Is everything okay?" Chef Brown asked as Shianne neared him.

"I don't know." She dashed behind Gregory.

Gregory sat on the couch, his hands covering his face.

She sat next to him and put her arms around his shoulders. "What's going on, honey?"

Gregory wiped his eyes with his hand. "I got laid off."

Shianne's gaze locked with his. Her heart sank. "Why?"

"Remember, I'd told you there were rumors about layoffs before we opened the bakery."

She nodded. "Ah, honey. How many people did they let go?"

"I don't know." He rubbed his face and eyes with his hands again.

"Did Tom lose his job?"

He shook his head. "No."

"What about Bob? Did they let him go too?"

Gregory looked upward. "No. They're keeping Bob."

"Oh, but they fired you?" Her voice rose. "How can they justify that? The optics on this looks horrible." Shianne kissed him on the cheek. "You'll find another job, a better job."

"I helped turn that company around in the short time I've been there. Now they want to get rid of me." He shook his head. "I'm having a hard time wrapping my head around this, baby."

"Sometimes, when situations like this happen, God is making way for something bigger and better."

Though Gregory was a man of God, Shianne's explanation wasn't what he wanted to hear.

"I have all the faith in the world that you'll get another job," Shianne said. "And I want you to exercise your faith as well. Besides, they weren't paying you what you're worth anyway."

"That's for certain. If I'd known the company was going to lay me off after such a short time here, I wouldn't have put in those extra hours every week."

"You give one hundred and ten percent. That's your character. You can't change that."

"Yeah, and look where it's brought me." He frowned.

"Don't beat yourself up. Your work principle has taken you far. Nothing's wrong with giving your best." Shianne rubbed her palm across his shoulder several times. "We're okay, honey. We've got money in the bank, and the bakery is doing fine." She smiled. "I'd love seeing you here at the bakery. You can help us out when you're not interviewing." Shianne hugged him. "Let's be thankful for what we have. We're current with our mortgage and car payments. The business is keeping me so busy that I don't have time for a vacation. My family and Scrumptious have me happier than ever. Don't worry. It'll be okay. We've lost money and gained money, and we've lost jobs and found better jobs."

He groaned. "My severance package includes six months of pay. Hopefully, I'll have a job by then."

"I want you to take some time to shake the dust from under your feet and then get back in the game. Re-invent yourself if you have to. You're not in the fourth quarter of your life. Right?"

"Right. I have to trust things will be all right." He kissed her. "Thanks for being here for me."

She looked at him oddly. "I'm always here for you."

"I still want to thank you."

Shianne stood from the couch. "I'll make you some lunch." Shianne hurt for Gregory; she felt like crying. She knew how much he'd loved his job. "Jesus!" she exclaimed, walking out of the room.

CHAPTER NINE

It was near store closing when Shianne heard a familiar voice. *I know that laugh.* She listened intently.

"Yes, our banana pound cake is delicious," she heard Frederick say. "It's one of our most popular items. Would you like a sample?"

"Sure."

The room quieted.

"Mm, this is good," the customer said moments later. "I'd like one. I'd also like ten lemon and five raspberry tarts. My wife loves lemon tarts."

I know that voice.

"I'm sorry, but we only have five lemon tarts. Customers love our tarts as well." Frederick chuckled.

"Then throw in a few more raspberry tarts, please."

Frederick packaged the items and brought them to the counter. "Will this complete your order?"

"Yes, I believe I have enough."

"That'll be forty-six ninety-five."

Miles pulled his wallet from his pants pocket, withdrew a credit card, and handed it to Frederick.

By then, Shianne had left her office and into the bakery. She couldn't believe what she was seeing. She took a double-take. Her mouth opened.

Oh, my goodness. Miles! Shianne thought about returning to her office but instead shuffled toward him. Her stomach turned summersaults. The two stared at each other for moments before she said, "Miles."

He followed with, "Shianne. Hi. How are you?"

"I'm fine. And you?"

"I'm good. I'm good. I don't believe this. What a surprise. I heard you had moved away."

"Yes, I lived in St. Louis for a few years."

They stood awkwardly looking at each other, Miles rocking back and forth on his heels, Shianne rubbing her sweaty palms together.

Miles loosened his tie. "Do you work here?"

"Yes. Scrumptious is my bakery," Shianne said proudly.

"Fabulous! I knew I had tasted that banana cake before."

Shianne had made dozens of pound cakes for Miles when they dated.

"So, you did it. You always said you'd open a bakery one day. Congratulations." He eyed the half-eaten banana cake in his hand. "I'm happy for you."

"Thanks. And how are things with you? Are you still coaching?"

"Yes, I'm still at Northwestern."

Shianne noticed sweat beading on Miles's forehead. She wondered if he was as nervous about their meeting as she was.

"How long have you been here?" Miles asked.

"We've been open a few months."

"I hear people talking about this bakery all the time. Had I known it belonged to you, I would have been in sooner." He checked his watch. "My wife is hosting a book club tonight, and she asked if I would pick up some desserts for the group."

Miles speaking of having another wife threw Shianne off-kilter. "So you've remarried?"

"Yes. London and I have been married for close to two years now."

"Congratulations." She wondered if her compliment had sounded as awkward as it felt. "And how's Kira? I bet she's quite a little lady."

He grinned like a proud father. "Kira's eleven now and acts like she's thirty. She's a smart girl. Just like her mother."

Shianne's eyes glistened. "I'm sure she's just like Brandy."

"What about you? Are you married? Kids?"

"Yes, I'm married. We have a little girl. Kaiya. She's five."

"So, you've been married for some years yourself?"

"Yes, a few years."

Frederick handed Miles his credit card along with a receipt and two pastry boxes. "Enjoy."

"Thanks, man." He turned back to Shianne. "It was nice seeing you. You look great."

She pushed back her hair. "So do you. Take care."

Shianne's heart beat faster as he walked out of the bakery. Her gaze followed him until he was out of sight.

"Is he an old friend?" Frederick asked.

"Yes. We went to college together."

"I bet it was great seeing him again."

"Yes. Nice." Shianne hurried to her office, her thoughts racing. She picked up her cell from the desk, called Michelle, and spoke before Michelle could finish her greeting. "Girl, you won't believe who just left the bakery."

"Hey, I was about to call you. Do I have time to run over and pick up some soup and my favorite sandwich?"

"Yes, come over. I'll have it waiting for you."

"Thanks. So, who came to the bakery?"

"I'll tell you when you get here."

"I'll be there in fifteen."

Shianne clicked off the phone, her thoughts surrounding her conversation with Miles.

When Michelle arrived twenty minutes later, Shianne had a tray of goodies waiting for her. "Let's go to my office. I don't want anyone thinking we're still open."

Michelle followed, and they sat at a round table across from Shianne's desk. Michelle eyed the food, smiling. "I appreciate this. I didn't feel like cooking."

Shianne chuckled. "Girl, please, you don't cook."

"Whatever." Michelle grabbed the sliced sandwich. "So, who's the mystery person who came into the bakery today?"

Shianne slapped the table. "Miles, girl. Miles."

"Miles?" Michelle laid her sandwich on the plate. "Really!"

"Yes! I wouldn't joke about something like this. He shocked the heck out of me. He came in to buy pastries for his wife."

"Wife? He's married again?"

Shianne leaned back in the chair. "Yep."

"This is crazy. How does Miles look?" Michelle bit into her sandwich.

"He's gained a little weight, but he looks great." Shianne thought about how fine she thought he was when they first met.

Michelle leaned closer. "What was it like seeing him again? I bet you almost peed yourself."

Shianne took a deep breath. "I was in the office when I heard this familiar voice talking to Frederick. I got up to see who it was, and it was Miles. Girl, I flipped. I wanted to turn around, but he saw me."

"What did you say?"

"What could I say but 'hi'?"

Michelle took another bite. "How's Kira? Did he mention her? She has to be about ten now?"

"Eleven. Miles smiled big when he talked about her. He's so proud of her."

"Did he ask what's going on with you?"

"I told him about Gregory and Kaiya. If he puts two and two together, I'm toast."

"What do you mean?"

She took her hand and pretended to shoot herself in the head. "My big mouth. I told Miles that Gregory and I have been married for a few years. Ki is five, Michelle! If he puts one and one together . . ."

Michelle held her glass in front of her lips. "He probably didn't pay any attention to all the details. I bet he was just as nervous seeing you."

Shianne shook her head. "Miles pays attention to everything. I hope he never comes here again."

Michelle's phone rang, and she retrieved it from her purse. "It's Erica. Let's tease her. She's always complaining we're doing things without her." She cleared her throat and answered. "Hey, girl. I'm at the bakery having a bowl of soup."

"What? And you guys didn't call me? Put Shianne on the phone."

Michelle whispered, "She wants to talk with you."

Shianne nodded.

Michelle pressed the icon. "You're on speaker."

"Why didn't you invite me over, Shianne?"

"I had to feed her. You know she doesn't cook. She looked hungry." Shianne laughed.

"Yeah, okay. Well, lucky for you girls, I'm meeting Aaron in a few minutes."

"So, why are you complaining? Where are you guys going?" Michelle asked.

"To dinner and a movie."

"Who's starring in the movie? You and Aaron?" Shianne asked, laughing.

"Girl, bye. I'll talk with you ladies later."

Michelle clicked off the phone and continued her conversation with Shianne. "Miles didn't waste any time getting remarried."

"I know, right?" Shianne said.

"That was sad about Brandy dying of cancer."

"I felt terrible for him when she died. I called and gave him my condolences. Ki was about two then. No way could I tell him about her while he was grieving about his wife."

Michelle sat back in her chair, looking as if she were in deep thought. "Miles resurfaces after five years. Imagine that? Suppose—"

Shianne waved her index finger. "No, no, no. There are no supposes."

"I agree. Both of you are married. But what if you weren't?"

"There is no what if. I'm not walking down that street with you."

"Did any of those old feelings resurface when you saw him?"

"Michelle! Why would you ask such a thing?"

"Did any anger flare up in you?"

"No. Nothing."

"I wonder how I'd feel if I ran into Brandon today. I don't

think I'd be mad at him, but I wouldn't have much to say to him."

"You haven't had as much time to heal over the relationship as I have. And I'm married. Happily married."

"Speaking of Gregory, how are things with his job search?"

"He has an interview next week. It looks promising. He worked with this guy in St. Louis, who's now in charge of HR at a Chicago firm."

"Let's pray that Gregory gets the job."

"Yes. Gregory needs a job and bad. He's had the wind at his back for so long he's having a hard time dealing with not working. We don't talk like we use to. And when we do, he's biting my head off." She paused. "He got mad the other day when I left the milk out on accident."

"He's under a lot of stress, Shianne."

"I know he is—poor baby. But I'm doing everything I can to let him know I got his back. That he has my support."

"Have you been paying down the loan?"

"Yes! I paid it down several thousand dollars. If he found out about the loan, he'd go ballistic considering what's going on now."

Shianne leaned in closer to Michelle as if she was revealing a secret. "Gregory and I haven't had sex in a few weeks."

Michelle's eyes perked. "No screaming, 'I love you' in the bedroom? No meaningful conversation about whose time it is to get the water?"

Shianne shook her head. "Nope. Unfortunately."

Michelle whistled. "Things are bad. Sounds like a poor state of affairs at the White's house."

"What's more frightening is I think I smelled alcohol on his breath the other evening."

"He's not saying, Woe is me, Lord, and then drinking?"

"I hope not."

"Scrumptious is doing better than you guys anticipated. Remind him of that, and tell him to stop stressing."

"I did. I do. I try encouraging Gregory every day."

Michelle wiped her mouth with a napkin. "Sounds like you and Gregory need a date night."

Shianne sat back in her seat and put her baby finger into her mouth, thinking. "A date night?"

"Yes. You guys have been so busy—you with the bakery, him with finding a job—that you haven't had time for each other. When's the last time you guys went to a movie?"

Shianne shrugged.

"When's the last time you went out to dinner? I know you can cook, but the chef deserves a night off. I'd say at least once a week."

Shianne looked at the apron she was wearing. "You're so right. I'd love trading this pink and blue Scrumptious apron for a sexy black or red dress."

Michelle looked upward. "Now, you're talking. You deserve it, girl! Have a good time with your hubby. Turn down the lights and dance to Luther."

"Ooh, and Gregory is such a good dancer." She pointed her index finger at Michelle. "I'm talking to him tonight about it."

"Don't just bring it up. Demand it! I'll keep Kaiya on date nights and make sure she gets to school the next morning."

"Aw, that's so sweet of you. You'd do that for us?"

She grinned. "Sure I'll do this for you and Gregory if it'll help get your romantic sparks back."

"So, what's up with you and Darius? Are you making your way toward steamy?"

"Steamy, no, but Darius and I are having a lot of fun. And he's so sweet. He texts me every morning, wishing me a good day, and calls and prays with me at night before I go to bed."

"Aw, that is sweet."

Michelle smiled broadly. "Yes, it is."

Gregory was setting the table when Shianne got home. The pot roast had cooked all day in the slow cooker and was ready.

"Hey, honey," she said, kissing him on the lips. "How was your day?"

"It was okay. Kaiya, come and eat!" he yelled.

Kaiya raced into the kitchen. "Hi, Mommy. I didn't know you were here."

"Hey, baby. Mommy just got home," Shianne said, wiping her hands with a paper towel. Shianne kissed Kaiya's forehead and sat at the table. "How was your day?"

Kaiya talked a mile a minute about her school day, which included her teacher giving students a longer recess time.

After dinner, Gregory cleared the table and washed the dishes while Shianne helped Kaiya bathe and get ready for bed. She then drew a bath for herself. The water was so relaxing she momentarily fell asleep.

Gregory gently touched her seconds later. "Babe, you shouldn't fall asleep in the tub."

Shianne awoke from her short nap. "I was waiting for you. Get in."

Gregory undressed and settled in with her.

"We haven't done this in a while," Shianne said, leaning against him. "We haven't done a lot of things in a while. I've been busy at the bakery, and you're busy finding a job. It feels like we're brother and sister instead of husband and wife sometimes. You used to smile when I walked in the room." She paused. "We need to set aside an evening a week for us. We can go to the movies, see a play, eat at a restaurant, or stay home and slow dance to Luther."

Gregory kissed her on the shoulder. "Sounds like a plan. Have you decided on a day?"

"Thursdays are good for me."

"Then Thursdays it is."

She nestled further into his arms. "Thanks, honey."

"I'm glad you brought this up because things have been a little crazy between us. I know I haven't been my best self. I'm trying not to let my not having a job interfere with us."

"You haven't been nice to me. You've been very un-Gregory-like. You haven't looked at me like I was your queen."

"I'm sorry. I always want you to feel special because you are. I wanted to talk to you about things, but you're having so much fun at the bakery. You're enjoying doing you. How can I interfere with that?"

Shianne's voice soured. "The bakery isn't my husband, Gregory."

"Sometimes, you act as if it is."

Shianne went silent. "I'm sorry if I made you feel that way," she said moments later. "I'm truly sorry." She kissed his hand. "Michelle said she'd babysit Ki on our date nights and take her to school the next morning."

He embraced her tighter. "That's great. Michelle is such a good friend to you."

"She's a good friend to the family, sweetie."

"Well, date night might be a night of just relaxing in the tub," he said, smiling.

"That's fine with me, honey. Just as long as we're together."

CHAPTER TEN

Michelle was over the moon with excitement that her favorite cousin, Paul, was visiting for the Thanksgiving holiday. She hadn't seen him in a year.

"Chelle!" he called out as he approached her with open arms.

"Hey, cousin."

He gave her a bear hug.

"You look great," she said, glossing over his muscular frame. *Erica's going to flip when she sees him.*

"Thanks, cousin. So do you. I've missed you, girl."

"I've missed you too. Are you hungry?"

"Yes."

"There's a nice Italian restaurant nearby." She picked up his duffle bag while Paul grabbed his suitcase, and they headed out of the airport.

About twenty minutes later, they entered the restaurant, and the hostess seated them.

"How's the business going?" Paul asked, perusing the menu.

"Things are going well. I wish I could hire someone to help me with marketing. I would have more time to design."

"I have a friend in Portland who's opening a grocery store. Maybe you can get your cards in his store. I'll call him."

"Thanks, cousin. That would be great."

He laid down the menu. "What else is happening with you? Who's the new boyfriend?"

"I don't have a boyfriend."

"That's not what Erica said."

Michelle set down her menu. "She has such a big mouth. When did you talk to Erica?"

"A few days ago."

"Does Marilyn know you're still having conversations with your ex-girlfriend?"

"Erica and I are just friends. We talk on occasion."

"Who calls whom?"

He smiled. "So, what's his name?"

"You're asking a question with a question?" She laughed. "Darius."

Paul sliced a piece of French bread and dipped it into a dish of olive oil. "Tell me about him. What does he do for a living?"

"He's an engineer, like you."

"Really? Is he good to you? Does he take you places? Does he spend those engineer dollars on you?"

"Paul!"

He chuckled. "I'm just asking."

"You'll get a chance to meet him soon. I've invited him to Thanksgiving dinner. I think you'll like him."

Paul rubbed his hands together. "This will be fun."

Michelle leaned closer. "You don't have to intimidate my men friends anymore."

"What do you mean?"

"You know how you've always tried scaring them away."

"I did not. I just did or said things to let them know I was watching them."

"Well, thank you, but it's no longer needed."

"We'll see."

Following lunch, Michelle went to the washroom. When returning to her table, she spotted Darius across the room, sitting with a woman. Michelle thought little of it, as Darius' office was nearby. She figured the lunch was business-related. But, as Michelle walked closer toward him, she noticed the woman was Carolyn. She wanted to turn around, but it was too late. Darius had seen her. *Okay, Michelle, pull yourself together.*

Darius smiled but appeared uneasy as Michelle approached his table. "Hey."

"Hi," Michelle responded.

Darius looked at Carolyn and then at Michelle.

"Hey, Carolyn," Michelle said.

"Hi, Michelle."

Carolyn was an attractive girl with a short curly afro and beautiful dimples.

"Carolyn and I are having lunch," Darius said.

Michelle gestured her head in the direction of her table. "I'm having lunch with my cousin, Paul. Remember, I told you I was picking him up from the airport today?"

Darius nodded. "Yeah. Yeah."

Silence fell among them. Michelle felt uncomfortable standing at the table with no one saying anything. Her body temperature warmed at Darius's strange behavior. "Well, I'll let you two finish your lunch."

"See you, Michelle," Carolyn said.

Darius stood and called after Michelle as she strode away, but Michelle ignored him. He caught up with her at her table.

"Did I miss something?" she asked.

"No. No, you didn't."

"Paul, this is Darius. Darius, this is my cousin Paul."

Paul put down his glass of water and shook his hand. "What's up, man?"

Michelle eyed Carolyn, who was taking in the scene.

Darius turned to Michelle. "She called and asked if I would meet her for lunch. She said she had something important to talk to me about."

"Oh, okay," Michelle said, not wanting to appear bothered by seeing them together.

Darius cleared his throat. "Let's talk later. Okay?"

"Sure." Michelle grabbed her coat from the chair and brushed past Darius as she headed for the door. She raced to her car with Paul following. Paul was hardly inside the vehicle when Michelle sped off.

"Okay, Chelle, you can slow down now," he said, strapping his seat belt. "What's going on?"

Michelle took a deep breath. "He's having lunch with his old girlfriend."

Paul shrugged. "I don't mean to sound glib, but I've had lunch with several of my girlfriends after we broke up. It's no big deal. It could be innocent."

"Well, why was he acting so weird if it's innocent?"

Paul shrugged. "I don't know. What was he doing that was so weird?"

"He acted like he was afraid to say anything. He wasn't acting like himself." Michelle held the steering wheel tighter as she turned a corner. She wondered if she'd overreacted and made a fool of herself in front of Paul.

Darius called ten minutes later. She clicked on the car phone.

"Michelle, we need to talk," he said with a sense of urgency in his voice. "I don't want you thinking the wrong thing. It isn't how it looked."

"What do you mean, *how it looked?* It looks like you were having lunch with your ex-girlfriend, that's all."

"I'm heading home. Meet me at my house in an hour. I'll tell you everything."

"You don't have to explain anything."

"Yes, I do. I want to. I'll see you in a few."

Michelle clicked off her phone and looked at Paul. "I'm not going."

"How can you find out what's going on if you don't hear the man out? I'll wait for you at Auntie's."

"Okay, but I shouldn't be gone longer than an hour. Then we can pick up Erica. I'm sure Mom and Dad are at home. They've been cooking for Thanksgiving dinner all week."

Driving to her parents' home, Michelle asked Paul not to say anything about them running into Darius. Not that he would anyway. Michelle's parents were in the kitchen, her mother stirring a pot of greens on the stove while her father marinated chicken.

"Hey, Aunt Samantha," Paul said, embracing her. "You're as pretty as ever."

Samantha blushed and ran her fingers through her hair. "You look great yourself. I swear it seems like you get taller every time I see you."

He grinned. "No, I'm still six-two, Auntie." He then turned to his uncle. "Uncle Earl, you look good, man."

The two embraced, and everyone sat at the table. Paul briefed everyone on what was happening back home as Michelle's thoughts wandered to her upcoming meeting with Darius. She was frightened by what might come from their talk. She was attracted to Darius and didn't want things to end between them.

"Hey, I have to go to the post office before it closes," she said, clutching her purse from the table. "I'll be right back, Paul."

"All right. Maybe I can convince Uncle Earl to give me the recipe for his barbecue sauce while I'm here."

Earl chuckled. "You'll have to do a lot of convincing."

Michelle stopped midway and turned around. "Don't snack too much, Paul. Remember, we're having dinner with Erica later. Besides, we just finished lunch."

Paul pointed at one of several cakes lined on the counter. "I have to get a least one slice of Aunt Samantha's chocolate cake. Forget what you're talking about, Chelle."

Michelle waved goodbye and left.

Extreme nervousness crept over Michelle as she drove to Darius's. Her heart raced, and her palms felt sweaty on the steering wheel. "Okay, Michelle, relax." She drew in slow, deep breaths until she reached his house.

Darius was standing on the porch when she pulled into the driveway. He strode to the car and opened the door. Michelle exited the car and leaned against it as if she wanted to talk outside, but Darius took her hand and led her into the house. Soft jazz played in the background.

"I made coffee," he said, leading her into the kitchen.

Michelle took a seat at the table.

"Would you like any cream or sugar?" he asked, as he poured her a cup and placed it before her.

"I'll drink it black." Michelle studied his face as he took a seat beside her. Darius looked worried. *Oh Lord, what is he going to say?*

Darius cleared his throat. "Carolyn says she pregnant. That's why she wanted to meet."

"Pregnant?" Michelle's voice rose an octave. Her heart pumped as if she had run a mile. She frowned and asked, "Is the baby yours?"

He shrugged. "I don't know. It could be. We saw each other a few times after we broke up."

She gasped. "You had sex a few times after you broke up is what you're saying, right?"

He sighed deeply. "Yes."

"So, what does this mean for you and me?"

He looked sadly into her eyes. "I hope nothing. I'm not getting back with her just because she's pregnant."

"Is this what Carolyn wants you to do? She knows about us, right?"

"Yes. I told her about you at lunch."

"How many months pregnant is she?"

"She said four months."

Her brow furrowed. "What? We've been together for three! Why did she wait so long to tell you?"

Darius fiddled with his mug. "I don't know. She couldn't answer that question."

"Did you see her after we started dating?"

"No! No! No! I swear. I fell for you the moment I saw you. You walked into that restaurant and stole my heart, Michelle. I couldn't go back to her." Darius sipped his coffee and rested the mug on the table. "She said she hadn't been with anyone since we broke up."

"Do you believe her?"

"I don't know. One thing I do know is I don't want this to come between us."

Michelle gave him a cold stare. "Will you take a paternity test?"

"I guess so."

"You guess so?" She rolled her eyes. "Man, what is wrong with you? I think you should. Unless …"

"I don't want her." He reached for Michelle's hand and held it. "I have no feelings for her. I want a relationship with you."

Michelle swallowed hard. She wished she could have camouflaged her feelings more and said something encouraging like, 'Oh, baby, we'll get through this.' But she couldn't. She was devastated.

"Darius, so many thoughts are running through my mind right now. We've had a lot of fun together. But how can you expect me to—" Michelle struggled to dam her tears.

"I understand," he said, still holding her hand. "I've thrown a lot at you today. I can only imagine how you're feeling. I made a big mistake. No doubt about it. I'm so sorry."

"Let's suppose the baby is yours. Then what?"

He squeezed her hand. "Then he or she is my child, and I'll help take care of it. You don't want to be with a man who doesn't take care of his child, Michelle, and I don't want to be an absent father." He leaned back. "My father worked all the time. He spent little time with my brothers and me. Sure, he wanted the best for us, but he was never around to do anything with us. My mother did everything. She attended our games, took us shopping for tennis shoes. We wanted Dad there. I swore if I had kids, I would be there for them."

Michelle knew he was right. She was fortunate to have both of her parents and believed no child should be without them.

"She just sprang this on you today?" she asked sternly.

"Yes, today is my first time hearing about the pregnancy."

She eyed him skeptically. "Are you sure?"

"Yes, baby. Yes."

Michelle clutched her purse. "I don't know what to say, Darius."

The thought of Darius having a baby with another woman sliced her gut. Her lips trembled. "I expect you to do what's right for the baby, even if it means being without me. I believe in fathers taking care of their children. You have no gripe from me about that. I don't know if continuing to see you is the best decision for me. I don't know if our relationship is strong enough to handle this. You're asking me to do something I might not be capable of doing." Michelle stood from the table. "You were supposed to be different. You were my fairytale," she said, leaving the room.

"I'm still your fairytale," he said, following her. "Just trust me." Darius followed Michelle to her car and held her.

Michelle's arms went limp around him. "I hope you can see things from my point of view." She slid into the car, and looking straight ahead, started the engine, and drove away.

Michelle sat parked outside her parents' home for several minutes before going inside. She wondered whether she should break up with Darius or support him. Her cell buzzed; the screen displayed it was Erica.

"Hey, girl," Erica said, her voice full of excitement. "When are you guys coming? I'm hungry."

"Sure you are," Michelle said, thinking Erica was eager to see Paul.

"What do you mean by that?"

"We're leaving soon. I took Paul to see Mom and Dad."

"All right. Tell everybody I said hello."

"Will do. See you in a few." Michelle clicked off the phone and went inside her parents' home, where everyone was watching TV.

"Hey, baby," her father said. "We expected you back a while ago."

"The lines at the post office were horrendous."

"I left you a small plate of greens in the oven, " Samantha said. "They're delicious."

"Thanks, Mama. I'll take them home with me." She looked over at Paul. "I hope you haven't stuffed yourself."

Her parents laughed as Paul shook his head.

"Stop lying," Michelle said, stepping from the room.

Paul followed her to the kitchen. "How did it work out?"

Michelle pulled the plate from the oven and shook her head. "You won't believe it." She sat at the table.

He sat beside her. "Tell me what happened."

Michelle uncovered the wrapped plate and sniffed the aroma. "Why does crazy shit always happen to me?"

"What's going on, Chelle?"

"Carolyn's pregnant," she said, recovering the plate.

Paul whistled and stroked his goatee. "Is it his?"

"There's a good chance. The man was having sex with her after they broke up."

Paul rubbed her shoulder. "That sucks. What are you going to do about it?"

She sighed. "I don't know. I like Darius. I like him a lot. Now he springs this crap on me."

Paul rested his elbows on the table. "Do you believe he's not seeing her anymore?"

She nodded. "I believe him. But I don't know if I want to be with a man who has a baby on the way."

Paul ran his hand down the side of his face. "Will he take a paternity test?"

"I suggested he do so."

"Suppose the child is his? You'll have to come to terms with it if you want to be with him."

Michelle knew Paul was right, but she wasn't ready to make a concession. "Oh, I'm the one who should compromise?"

"Well, what else can you do? You can't act like the baby doesn't exist. I know you're not that heartless."

She sniffed. "No, I'm not, but I'm not the bad guy in this. He got her pregnant. He's the one who couldn't keep his stuff in his pants." She wiped tears from her eyes.

"I'm sorry, Chelle."

"Let's pick up Erica. This situation won't get resolved tonight." She paused. "I didn't tell you Erica knows Carolyn, that they work together, so don't mention this to her tonight, okay? I don't need to hear her mouth." Michelle sighed. "This is freakin' unbelievable."

Erica opened the door, smiling as if someone had given her a Chanel bag.

"You look stunning," Paul said, giving her body a full look over.

Erica wore a white sweater over a pair of black leggings. A bronze necklace draped her neck.

"Turn around, girl." He took her hand and twirled her. "You get finer every time I see you." He kissed her on the cheek.

Erica blushed. "You don't look too shabby yourself."

Despite their denial, Michelle felt Erica and Paul still had feelings for each other.

Paul surveyed the spacious living room. "You've done some remodeling since I was last here. The place looks great."

Erica grinned and pointed at the new windows. "My latest remodeling project. Aren't they great? I just love them."

He glanced at the arched ceiling. "And you have new light fixtures too, huh?"

Michelle stretched out on the couch and watched them as they chatted. *Enough of this already.*

Erica smiled. "How long are you going to be here? I could use your help with a few things. I want to change the bathroom vanity."

He smiled and eyed Michelle. "Do you hear her, Chelle?"

"Ah, come on," she said, stroking his hand. "I'll help you as much as I can."

"Yeah, right," Michelle said under her breath.

"I guess I can help you," Paul said. "It'll get me out of Michelle's hair when she's working."

"Great! Come, let me show you." She took his hand and led him upstairs as Michelle lay on the couch, staring at the ceiling. Erica and Paul returned several minutes later.

"What were you guys doing up there?" Michelle asked. "It doesn't take that long to look at a sink."

"Girl, hush!" Erica said.

"Nah, you hush, Erica." *If Marilyn knew what her fiancé was up to tonight.*

Paul gave a puzzled look.

"I'll get my coat," Erica said. "I'm so hungry."

Michelle stood. "No, you're thirsty."

Erica blew off the remark and pulled her coat from the closet.

Later, after enjoying dinner at a new seafood restaurant in town the three went to a place called Marvin's for live music. Marvin's had a lively vibe, which relaxed Michelle some, but Darius wasn't off her mind entirely. By the time Michelle dropped Erica off at home, she felt as if she would explode.

"I'm so angry, Paul. Why did he keep seeing her when he knew it was over?" She took a deep breath. "What's with you, men?"

"What do you mean?"

"If they broke up, why did they continue to have sex?"

"I don't know. Sometimes when a couple breaks up, it's hard to let go. I'm not saying this is what happened with Darius and Carolyn. But breaking up isn't always easy."

"What should I do?"

He exhaled a deep sigh. "I hate seeing you go through this. I guess if you like the guy and believe he's telling the truth, you'll make it work. Follow your heart."

"I believe him." She sighed. "I can't say how I'll act when she calls talking about 'the baby needs this' or 'the baby needs that' or 'can you come over. This is so hard. I know one thing, he'd better take a paternity test, or I'm out."

"There are other guys."

"I know. But I like this guy."

"Why don't you invite him over to watch the game with us today?

I'd like to get to know him."

She cracked a smile. "What, you plan to interview Darius during halftime?"

Paul chuckled. "No. I want to hang out with the guy who has my cousin's heart. Why not?"

"Um, I don't know. We'll see."

"What can it hurt, Chelle?"

Michelle lay in bed, contemplating Paul's suggestion. She grabbed her phone from the nightstand and, though it was after 1 a.m., she texted Darius and invited him to watch the game with her and Paul. She felt extremely nervous after pushing the send button.

Darius responded immediately with a call. His deep, velvety voice excited her. "Yes, I'd love to watch the game. Thanks for the invite. Do you want me to bring anything?"

She smiled. "No, I have everything. We'll see you around one, okay?"

"Sure."

She grinned, thinking how riled up Paul got over his favorite sports teams. "I hope you're a Packers fan, because, if you aren't, Paul will have a field day with you."

He laughed. "Packers fan, I am not. Tell Paul to bring it on."

Uh-oh.

"This should be fun, Michelle. Thanks for inviting me," he said softly.

The two said goodnight, and Michelle clicked off the phone. She loved that Darius had called her instead of responding by text. She wanted to hear him unfiltered and honest—no first drafts. No emojis. He said she was special, and she wanted to see it in his actions.

CHAPTER ELEVEN

Michelle awakened in a crummy mood, no longer excited about Darius watching the game with her and Paul. *Jesus, what am I going to do about this man?* She snatched her cell from the nightstand and called him.

"Good morning, baby," he said.

"Darius, I was thinking, let's take a break for now. I'm not saying I want to end things between us, but I need time to reconcile what's going on."

"This isn't what I expected to hear from you this morning, Michelle. I woke up excited to see you today."

Michelle didn't respond.

"I understand you need time to digest what's before us, but we can work this out without distancing ourselves from each other."

"No, we can't. At least I can't. And, as for today, I'll tell Paul I changed my mind about having you over."

"Michelle…"

She clicked off the phone.

Hours later, while making snacks for the game, the doorbell rang. Michelle wiped her hands and answered the door.

"Hey," Darius said with a twisted smile on his face.

"I thought…" she said, her voice crackling.

"I'm sorry, but I need to talk to you. Can I come in? I'd be kicking myself if I didn't try to see you."

Michelle stood in the doorway, not saying anything.

"We have to talk Michelle."

After several moments, Michelle swung open the door, and he walked inside. Casually dressed in a pair of jeans and a beige leather jacket, Darius looked as if he had come from a photo shoot for Bianca Saunders.

"Paul's already sitting in front of the TV."

Michelle took his coat and draped it on a chair before going into the family room.

Paul gave a surprised gaze. "Hey, man, you're just in time." He stood from the La-Z-Boy and shook Darius's hand. "Are you ready for some football?"

Darius sat on the couch. "Yeah, I guess."

Paul grinned. "Are you a Packers fan?"

"Are you crazy? I'm Bears all the way." He eyed Paul's green and white Packers jersey and hat.

"Man, get out of here," Paul said, grabbing a potato chip from a bowl and popping it into his mouth.

This should be interesting, Michelle thought, leaving the room. Moments later, she returned with a platter of chicken wings and dip. She placed them on the table, but Paul took the plate and set it on his lap.

"Man, give me some of those wings," Darius said, chuckling. He took five or six wings and placed them on a saucer.

"I thought you made the wings for me, Chelle," Paul said. "You know I love your hot honey wings."

"I made enough for everyone, Paul."

Paul placed the platter on the nearby table, dished several wings onto his plate, and licked his fingers. "Mm, I wish Marilyn could make wings like you, Chelle."

"Now, that's one thing Marilyn and I have in common. We don't cook."

"Yeah, but you can cook," Paul said, grinning. "Marilyn, can't cook."

Michelle laughed. "I'm telling her you were ragging on her cooking."

Paul bit into a wing. "She knows she can't cook."

Michelle listened to the male bonding between Paul and Darius as they watched the game. She could see Paul liked Darius, which made her feel better. Not only did they talk about football, but they chatted about their careers and other things.

During halftime, Michelle received a call from her mother. She'd reconnected with a cousin on the internet and wanted to share the good news with Michelle. They hadn't talked to each other in over ten years, and her mother was thrilled. Michelle went into another room so she wouldn't disturb the guys.

Paul leaned forward to confirm Michelle was out of earshot. "Hey, man, I hear you have quite a situation going on."

Darius gave a puzzled look. "She told you?"

"Of course, she did. We talk about everything."

"Yes, it's bad, man. This lady I was dating says she's pregnant."

"Was that the young lady you were in the restaurant with?"

He nodded. "Yes, unfortunately."

"Man, Michelle likes you, but I don't know if she likes you enough to stay with you through this."

He frowned. "I've put Michelle in a very awkward place, I know. The last thing I want to do is hurt her. I'm afraid she'll let this come between us."

"My advice is to take the paternity test, and if the child is yours, assure her the baby won't change things between you two. Let her know you've got her. And she'll need to hear it more than once."

"If I could change things, I'd do it in a heartbeat. I'm crazy about Michelle, man. I've never met anyone like her."

"Have you told her that?"

"Yes. I've told her several times."

"Well, it looks like you have to keep telling her."

When Michelle returned to the room, halftime was over. Darius and Paul were into the game, yelling and screaming at the players as they attempted to score.

"Who's winning?" she asked, sitting on the couch with Darius.

"Chicago," he said, hugging her.

After the game—in which Chicago beat Green Bay 10-6— Erica called Paul and asked him to come over. Now alone, Michelle and Darius played a few sets of spades before Darius summoned enough courage to mention Carolyn and the baby.

"Michelle, I'm so sorry. It kills me that I'm putting you through this. I made a terrible mistake getting with Carolyn after we had broken up."

"Hearing another woman is pregnant by a man you're dating is something no woman wants to go through. It's hard, Darius. Pregnancy doesn't just happen. You continued having sex with her after you broke up?" She sighed. "You guys didn't use birth control?"

"No. Carolyn told me she couldn't get pregnant."

Michelle raised an eyebrow. "And you believed her?"

"I feel silly now, but yes, I believed her."

"I was so excited about us, Darius. Have you heard from her since the other day?"

He laid his cards on the table. "She called this morning. I told her I wanted a paternity test."

"What did she say?"

"Nothing I want to repeat."

"What did she say?"

"She yelled and cursed me out. She also said some hateful things toward you. I told her you had nothing to do with me not wanting her."

Michelle stood from the chair and went to the window, captured by the season's first snowfall. The blanketing snow sprinkled like diamonds in the yard. Darius joined her, wrapping his arms around her waist.

"When I was a little girl, my mother would make ice cream from the snow. She'd set a large bowl outside the back door, and once the bowl was full, she'd bring it inside and add a few teaspoons of vanilla flavoring, a little milk, and sugar to it." She smiled. "It was so good."

Darius smiled. "What a great memory."

Michelle faced him. "I'm glad you decided to take the test. Then there'll be no doubts."

"And if the baby is mine, then what?"

"We'll deal with it. Though I have mixed feelings about it all, it's not like you cheated on me outright. You were together before I came along. I have to trust what you say until you show me otherwise."

Darius sighed loudly. "Thank you! I don't want to lose you over this." He paused. "So, we're good?"

She nodded. "I believe so." Michelle hadn't asked Darius much about his relationship with Carolyn. She wondered if Darius had loved her. "I have a question, and I hope you'll answer it."

He studied her face. "You can ask me anything, baby."

"Did you love her?"

"No. No, I didn't. I cared about her, but I didn't love her. I can say it with forthrightness because my feelings for her don't compare to how I feel about you. I liked Carolyn. I adore you." Darius reached for her and passionately kissed her. "I promise you won't regret being with me. One thing I don't do is lie. I'll always be upfront with you, Michelle."

Michelle lay in bed with her eyes closed, thinking about Darius. Unable to sleep, she decided she'd go to her office and work. Paul peeked into the room an hour later.

"You're still up?"

Michelle stopped typing. "Yes. I'm getting a little work done. I couldn't sleep."

Paul parked on the loveseat. "So, how's Michelle and Darius?"

"We're not where I'd like us to be. But we're okay."

"So I take it you and Darius are straight on the DNA test?"

"Yes."

Paul nodded. "Sounds like a plan. He seems like a decent brother, Chelle."

"I believe he is. That's why I've decided to ride it out." Michelle checked the time on her computer. "It's kind of late for you to be getting back. What were you and Erica up to?"

He was silent for a moment. The silence wasn't like Paul, Michelle thought.

She swiveled the chair toward him. "What's going on with you and Marilyn? She called four times during the game."

He exhaled a deep sigh. "It's the wedding. She doesn't believe I was serious when I said I wanted to call it off."

Michelle's eyebrow rose. "You're calling off the wedding? Why?"

"Because I want to."

"I wondered why you weren't wearing your engagement ring. I just thought you didn't want to offend Erica."

He sighed again. "I don't think Marilyn's the woman for me. She's nice and all, but she's too needy. I can't be out of her sight for five minutes before she's calling me. I don't need that. I hate explaining my every move to her. I won't do that with anyone. I work long hours sometimes, and I don't need her badgering me when I get home. Either she trusts me, or she doesn't."

"Have you given her reason not to trust you?"

"No, I haven't," he said, removing his shoes.

Michelle looked at him wide-eyed, knowing he had been talking with Erica on the phone. He had said so himself. "Have you talked to her about it?" Michelle asked, biting her nail.

"Several times. I told her to stop stalking me, or we're finished."

"You gave her an ultimatum?"

"Yes."

Michelle sat frozen. "You know women don't like ultimatums. What did she say?"

"She didn't say anything, which led me to believe she didn't take me seriously."

Michelle leaned back in her chair. "Did you get your ring back?"

He shook his head. "No, she can keep it."

She looked at him as if he had two heads. "What? You're letting her keep the ring? It cost you a lot of money. Cousin, you don't give up a beautiful diamond ring so quickly."

He tilted his head. "Would you give it back if it were you?"

"Heck, no!"

He rested his head against the couch. "I don't want to fight with her about it. Should I fall in love again, I'll buy another ring. It's not like I hate the girl. I just can't spend the rest of my life with her." He stood and headed for the door. "Any wings left?"

"Perfect segue," Michelle said, following him.

Once inside the kitchen, Michelle withdrew a yogurt cup from the fridge while Paul put the wings in the microwave.

"What's going on with you and Erica?" Michelle asked. "She doesn't have anything to do with your breakup with Marilyn, does she?"

Paul sighed deeply. "I don't know. We still have feelings for each other, but I don't know if they're strong enough for us to get back together."

"You guys talked about it?"

"Mm-hmm, that's why I was over there so late. I told Erica if she loved Aaron, she should stick with him. Not to mess up their relationship because of me. We've tried being together, and it didn't work. Neither she nor I do long-distance dating well. And I'm not moving back here, and she's not moving to Oregon."

"If you have feelings for her, how can you suggest she stay in a relationship with another man? Come on, cousin."

He shook his head. "I don't know what'll happen between us."

Michelle dipped her spoon inside the cup and dished out the last spoonful of yogurt. "I'm going to bed."

"Goodnight. I'm going to watch a little TV before I turn in."

She patted his shoulder. "Don't stay up too late. You have real work at Erica's tomorrow. Goodnight."

"Are you being facetious?"

"Yes," she said, exiting the room.

Michelle lay in bed, feeling sorry for Marilyn. She thought about how devastated Marilyn must feel, knowing Paul didn't want to marry her. Michelle wasn't a big fan of Marilyn. She felt Marilyn was too pretentious, but, as a woman, she felt her pain. She wondered whether her sensitivity to Marilyn's plight was because of what she was going through with Darius.

Why does love have to be so complicated?

CHAPTER TWELVE

The clock read 9:30 a.m. Michelle had overslept, and on Thanksgiving morning, of all mornings. *Mama's probably thinking about sending Daddy over here.* Michelle had promised her mother she'd be at her house at nine that morning to help prepare for dinner that afternoon.

The phone rang, startling her. She covered her eyes with her hands. "I'm coming, Ma. I'm coming." Michelle grabbed her cell and answered.

"Happy Thanksgiving," Shianne's cheery voice said.

"Hey, girl."

"Are you at your mother's?"

"No, not yet. I overslept."

"Girl, you better get up. You know, Mama Samantha will not tolerate you being late." She chuckled. "Did you and Darius have a late night?"

"Kinda sorta."

"Did you have fun?"

"Yeah, I guess."

"Girl, what's going on with the vague answers?"

Michelle sighed. "Remember I told you about Darius and Carolyn dating?"

"Uh-huh."

"Well, I ran into them together at Spargo's the other day. Paul and I had gone there after I picked him up from the airport."

"What a coincidence. Was he surprised to see you?"

Michelle lightly tapped the bed with her hand. "He looked as if he'd seen a ghost when I walked over to their table."

"What were they doing together? I hope he had a good explanation."

"Darius didn't have too much to say at the time. Carolyn and I made small talk, and then I went back to our table. He must have felt bad about how he acted, because he called me shortly after we left the restaurant, asking that I meet him at his house later."

"So, what did he say? You did go?"

"She's pregnant!"

Shianne gave a screeching, "Pregnant!"

"Girl, can you believe that? It hit me like a ton of bricks." Michelle covered her eyes with her hand again.

Shianne moaned. "How many months is she?"

"He said four months. I felt sick to my stomach."

"I'm sorry. I know how much you like Darius."

Michelle exhaled. "I do. I like him a lot. I'm so hurt."

"Sure, you are. Any woman in her right mind would be."

"I like that he's willing to take care of the baby if it's his, but I'm not about the baby mama drama."

"Wait a minute. Darius isn't sure the baby is his?"

"No, but he believes it might be his child. They had broken up but continued to have sex."

"Good ole, 'We can't be together, but we can still have sex.'"

Michelle pointed her index finger into the air. "You got it."

"Well, it sounds like he needs to take a paternity test."

Michelle nodded. "That's what I told him."

"What happens if he's the father?"

Michelle exhaled a loud sigh. "Then he's the father. There's nothing I can do about it. We talked about it, and Darius said he wouldn't be an absent father."

"I applaud him for that."

"So do I."

"Has Erica said anything about Carolyn being pregnant?"

"No. Maybe she doesn't know."

"Goodness. Just when you find a guy you like …"

"I know, right? I'm tired of getting caught up in somebody else's BS." Michelle pouted. "I didn't sign up for this. I don't know if I want or can be with a man who has a baby on the way."

"It's understandable. This reminds me of the situation between Miles and Brandy. I had no problem with Miles spending time with Kira because I knew he wanted to be in his daughter's life. But I didn't know Brandy was tagging along. They were at the beach, at restaurants, and other places together. I'm not saying she planned it that way, but their outings opened the door for other things to occur."

"That could happen with Darius and Carolyn, though he says he doesn't have any feelings for her."

"If you care about him and want to continue the relationship, I guess you have no choice but to believe him. But the mere hint that something is amiss, you call him on it. Don't wait forever, as I did. Follow your gut!"

"Oh, you can bet I will!" Michelle paused. "I just want to be in a stress-free relationship with a wonderful man." She outstretched her hands. "Is that too much to ask?"

"Life comes with its ups and downs, girlfriend. You know, I know."

The two sat silent for several moments.

"Well, let me get dressed before Mama knocks at my door."

Shianne laughed. "I'm surprised she's not there already."

Michelle laughed with her. "Bye. I'll see you guys in a few hours." She jumped out of bed, showered, and hurried over to her mother's.

Excitement filled the Anthony residence. Samantha had decorated her home holiday style in colors of red, brown, orange, and yellow. Apple cinnamon scented the air as holiday music played in the background. An ensemble of appetizers including deviled eggs, hot spinach and artichoke dip, crab-stuffed mushrooms, bacon-wrapped Brussels sprouts with lemon dip, holiday cheeseballs, and fresh onion dip with veggies displayed on beautiful platters in the living and dining rooms.

"Thanks for helping with the appetizers, Shianne," Samantha said, gleaming. She reached for a mushroom. "I can't stop eating them. Girl, you know you can cook."

"They are good," Michelle said, reaching for another one.

"Anytime, Mama Samantha. We're happy for the invite, especially since my family no longer lives in Chicago."

The doorbell rang as they chatted.

"I'll get it," Michelle said, wiping her hands with a napkin. Michelle swung open the door, thinking she'd be greeting other guests, but it was Carolyn.

"Carolyn," she said, her voice cracking.

"Hey, Michelle. Is Darius here?"

"Um, what's going on?"

"Can I see him for a moment? I want to invite him to my parents' for Thanksgiving."

A blank expression flashed across Michelle's face. *What the hell!* "Carolyn, he's spending the holiday with me and my family and friends. This is my parent's house. I'm sure he would have called you had he wanted—"

"Darius!" Michelle yelled into the house. "Would you please come to the door, honey?"

Darius rushed to the door. "Yes, baby?"

Michelle nodded in Carolyn's direction and stepped aside.

"Carolyn? What are you doing here?"

"I wanted to invite you to Thanksgiving dinner, baby."

"Baby?" Michelle interrupted.

Darius lightly eased Michelle away a few steps. "First of all, I'm not your baby. And I'm where I want to be. How did you know I was over here? You got to go." He took Michelle's hand in his.

A sour look crossed Carolyn's face.

Seconds later, Michelle overheard her mother calling her.

"I'll be there in a minute, Ma!"

Within moments, Samantha came to the door. "Oh, we have more guests? Hi. I'm Mrs. Anthony, Michelle's mother. Happy Thanksgiving to you."

"Happy Thanksgiving to you too, ma'am."

"Carolyn was just leaving," Darius said, taking hold of the doorknob.

"You're more than welcome to share the holiday with us," Samantha said.

"Mama!"

"Come on in," Samantha said, leading her inside and ignoring her daughter's plea. Carolyn sauntered behind her.

"Michelle, would you please take her coat? Don't worry," she whispered to Michelle. "We'll kill her with kindness."

"Nah, Mama, there's no need for kindness! I'm going to put my foot up her . . ." Michelle reluctantly took her coat and hung it in the closet.

"Everyone, this is Carolyn," Samantha said, entering the living room.

Eyes widened, mostly in disbelief.

"Carolyn?" Erica said.

Shianne gave a peering expression, and her jaw dropped. "She has a lot of nerve," she whispered to Michelle.

"It's time for dinner. I hope everyone's still hungry after eating those delicious appetizers," Samantha said, breaking the ice.

"Yes, I'm ready to eat," Earl said, rubbing his hands together.

"Me too," Paul said.

Erica whispered in Carolyn's ear as the others left the room. "Can I talk to you for a minute?"

"Sure."

"Yeah, she better talk to her, because I don't do madness well," Michelle said to Shianne. "I'm nipping this mess in the bud today!"

Erica waited for everyone to leave the room before having her fireside chat. "Carolyn, what are you doing here? What is wrong with you?"

"I came to talk to Darius about something."

Erica put her hands on her hips. "What could be so important that you come to his girlfriend's parents' home? Why didn't you call him?"

"I did, but he didn't answer his phone."

Erica slapped her hip with her hand. "That should have told you something! And let me guess— when he didn't answer your call, you decided to look for him here. You're crazy as hell! I know we're coworkers, but you're wrong for this. Don't bring my friend and her family into your bull."

Carolyn frowned. "This is not bull."

"Then what is it? What do you call it? Have some respect for yourself. If the man doesn't want to be bothered with you, move on." Erica shook her head. "Do you think you'll get him back by stalking him?"

Carolyn didn't respond.

Erica pointed a finger at her. "Now, I want you to go into that room and politely excuse yourself. I don't care what lie you make up, but you got to go. Do you understand what you just did? Do you know how silly you look? If you'd been somewhere else, you might have gotten your ass whooped. I might even …"

Erica led the way into the dining room with Carolyn following.

"Mrs. Anthony, I'm sorry, but I can't stay." Carolyn's voice quivered. "My mother called and said the family was having dinner earlier than planned, and that they're waiting for me."

"Ah. I was so looking forward to you joining us. Maybe next time."

"There will be no next time," Michelle said.

Shianne gnashed her teeth. "Yes, we were looking forward to you joining us, Carolyn. I wanted to chat with you."

"Michelle, would you get her coat?" Samantha asked.

Carolyn followed behind Michelle and Darius.

"What did you say to her?" Shianne mouthed to Erica.

"Nothing," she mouthed back and smiled.

"I don't know what you call yourself doing, Carolyn, but it stops here," Darius said, opening the door. "Don't ever do this again! How many times do I have to tell you, I don't want you! It's over between us."

Tears swam in Carolyn's eyes.

Michelle felt a tad uncomfortable. She hadn't seen Darius so angry before.

"I've told you I'd help with the baby if it's mine, but's that's as far as I go with you. Our relationship is over. You got it?" His mouth set in a hard line.

Carolyn sneered and left the house.

Darius watched her get inside the car and closed the door. He hugged Michelle. "I'm sorry, baby, she brought this nonsense to your mother's house."

"She's lost her freakin' mind?"

"It won't happen again. I promise you."

After dinner, the men settled in with a game of dominoes while the ladies cleared the table and chatted.

"What did you say to Carolyn?" Shianne asked Erica. "She trudged into the room, looking as if someone had threatened her. Her eyes were all big."

"I asked her if she thought crashing Thanksgiving dinner at her ex's girlfriend's parents' home would send him running back to her." She sighed. "I then told her to …"

"To what?" Samantha asked with a piercing eye.

Erica knew she had to pepper her conversation around Samantha. "To call an Uber if her car didn't start."

Everyone broke out laughing—even Samantha.

"An Uber?" Michelle screeched.

"Well, I think you handled things just fine," Samantha said, patting Erica's shoulder. "Good job."

"Thank you," she said, smiling appreciatively.

Samantha laid her dishcloth on the counter and left the room to join the others. The girls continued with the dishes.

"Now that Mama Samantha is out the room, I told Carolyn she was crazy as hell for coming over here, and she's lucky she didn't get her butt kicked. The girl has no shame."

"Thanks, girl," Michelle said, "Because sweet Michelle was ready to give up her nice-girl card. How did she know to come here or where Mom lives anyway?"

"Girl, you can find anything on the internet these days. She must have overheard me telling a coworker I was having Thanksgiving here."

"She had some nerve coming here," Shianne said, handing Erica a plate to dry. "Where's the girl's self-pride? Where is her dignity? Never would I embarrass myself like that."

"She might try other foolish things, now that she's pregnant, Michelle," Erica cautioned. "She might become psycho B. Dun dun dun dun!"

"I wish she would!" Michelle countered.

"Has she mentioned to anyone at work she's pregnant?" Shianne asked.

Erica nodded. "Yes, but she hasn't said Darius is the father."

"I wonder why not?"

"I don't know. Maybe Carolyn doesn't know who the father is."

Michelle winced. "Ouch!"

That night, as Michelle and Darius settled in her parent's family room, he apologized again for Carolyn's behavior. "I don't understand her. She calls my job and hangs up. Texts and emails me all the time. Now, she's bothering you. This is where I draw the line. I'll …"

"I'll what?" Michelle asked.

"I'll have her arrested the next time she comes around uninvited."

"Darius…" Michelle patted his hand.

"I will, baby. I will. I'm not dancing with Carolyn. Her messing with you is where I set the limit."

It felt satisfying that Darius was standing by her, but Michelle hoped Carolyn's antics would end. Michelle kissed him on the cheek and wrapped her arm around his shoulders. "Enough of this talk about Carolyn. It's still early, let's go hear some live music."

"Sounds like a good idea. It'll be a nice way to end the holiday."

CHAPTER THIRTEEN

Bakery

Shianne was uncertain what time the phone rang, but she knew it was the middle of the night. It had been date night for Gregory and her, and they hadn't made it home until after eleven from dinner and a movie.

"What do you mean?" Shianne overheard Gregory say. "We'll be right over."

Gregory nudged her hip lightly. "Baby, get up. That was the police. Someone's broken into the bakery."

Shianne sat upright, her eyes large, and her heart pounding. "My bakery? Someone's broken into my bakery?" she repeated. "What else did they say?"

"We'll learn more when we get there. Get dressed."

Shianne flung back the blankets and slid into the purple skirt and blouse she had worn earlier. She felt weak as she stumbled to the bathroom to wash her face. Shianne knew horrible things happen, sometimes in the nicest of neighborhoods, but she never expected it would occur at her Scrumptious Bakery. A few moments later, she wiped the toothpaste from around her mouth and hurried downstairs. Gregory was already in the car when she stepped outside.

Shianne tried stifling tears as Gregory drove to the bakery. Everything she had done throughout the years to prepare for the bakery ran through her head—saving money, buying equipment, arguing with Gregory.

"It'll be all right, Shianne. Don't worry, baby. It'll be all right," Gregory said trying to soothe her.

The sight of blinking red, white, and blue lights sent shockwaves through Shianne's body as they drove alongside the bakery. "Jesus!"

Gregory parked the car, and they rushed inside. Toppled tables and chairs, flour blanketing the floor, the cash register open, and the picture of Grandma Eva lying on the ground nauseated her.

Gregory approached one of the officers. "I'm Gregory White, and this is my wife, Shianne. We're the owners."

"I'm Officer Reed, the one who called you. As you can see, they trashed the place. The alarm went off around three a.m."

"Why would they wreck the bakery like this?" Shianne shook the shattered glass from the frame holding Grandma Eva's photo. "Wasn't breaking in enough?" Shianne then lifted an overturned table and placed two chairs under it.

"Was there any money in the cash register?" Officer Reed asked.

"Maybe a hundred dollars and some change," Shianne answered.

She turned to Gregory. "I deposited money in the bank yesterday. I'd thought about waiting until today because I wanted to get home early for dinner. I'm glad I followed my first mind and got it out the way."

"It also looks like they took some items from your refrigerators. They were open," Officer Reed said.

Shianne rushed to the kitchen to view for herself.

Gregory and Officer Reed followed behind.

"They've stolen deli food, chicken salad, even eggs. Now, who steals eggs?" Shianne asked with a confused look. "This is just crazy."

"It doesn't appear they got in through the back door, although it was open when a unit arrived." Officer Reed pointed to the ceiling. "We believe they got inside by sliding through those tiles."

Shianne looked upward and put her hands on her hips. "Really? This is insane. They should have slipped and broken their legs."

Officer Reed pointed to a wall-mounted security camera. "I'd like to see the videotape in your surveillance cameras. We'll check other cameras in the area also. Maybe they'll help lead to an arrest."

"I certainly hope so."

Shianne then rushed to her office. Papers were strewn across her desk. She picked up a few pieces of mail. "Some of these letters have our home address on it, Gregory." She exhaled deeply. "Suppose they try to break into our house."

He ran his hands through his hair. "We have a security system, baby. We also have video cameras and motion lights outside the house."

"We have a security system here, and they broke in. This is frightening."

"I know, baby."

Gregory turned to Officer Reed. "Do you think they'll try to break into our home?"

"I don't know. It sounds like you have a lot of things in place to lessen your chances of a burglary."

"While we don't have a dog, most of our neighbors have one or two. Our next-door neighbor has a pit bull they keep fenced outside. He barks at everything," Gregory said.

"Even so, I can't say they won't try to break into your home," Officer Reed said.

Shianne brushed her hand through her hair. "Let's clean up this place, Gregory. We're opening today, even if we have to open late. I'm not letting this incident keep us from moving forward. Our customers expect us to be open."

"We'll get it done. Let me call Max first, so he can send someone to inspect the ceiling. It might need repairing."

A slender, muscular officer with light brown hair came from the outside and into the office, dangling a multi-colored hat with a pink ball on top.

"Does this hat belong to anyone?"

Shianne shook her head. "It's not mine. It doesn't look familiar to me."

"We'll hold it as evidence," the officer said.

"It looks like a woman's hat," Shianne said.

"Your burglar could be a woman," Officer Reed replied. "Maybe she tagged along with her boyfriend or him with her. We've seen it all."

"Well, I'm happy no one got hurt," Shianne said. "Chef Brown and Frederick come in around four to bake."

"Yes, we're blessed." Gregory wrapped his arm around Shianne's shoulders. "This could have turned ugly."

Gregory and Shianne finished speaking with the officers and then started cleaning the bakery—Shianne with a broom in hand, Gregory, with a mop and bucket.

"Baby, you may not want to hear this, but I think you should get a gun," he said, wiping a table.

"A gun? A gun for what? I don't want a gun."

"You need to protect yourself. You leave here some nights when it's dark."

"Chef Brown or Frederick always walk me to my car."

Gregory tossed a rag into the pail and removed his gloves. "Well, at least apply for a FOID card. You can decide later about the gun."

Shianne sat in a chair and mulled Gregory's suggestion. "It's probably a good thing to do. I don't understand why people won't get a job instead of destroying what someone else has worked hard to build. Jobs are out there for anyone who wants to work."

"The problem is that not everyone wants to work."

Chef Brown and Frederick entered the bakery, wide-eyed and eager to hear what had occurred.

"Someone broke into the bakery," Shianne said.

Chef Brown took up a fighting stance. "I wish they had come in while I was here. They would have gotten a chance to meet Oliver." He regarded the green backpack in his hand.

"Oliver?" Shianne asked. "I hope Oliver is legal."

"Yes. I do everything by the book."

Her brow furrowed.

"I'm mad as heck. I want to punch someone in the face," Frederick said. "Things are going so good for us."

"They'll continue to go well for us." Shianne made eye contact with both of them, so they would understand the weight of what she was about to say. "If anybody ever comes in here to rob the bakery, you give them whatever they want." She fanned her hand across the room. "Everything in this bakery is disposable. Your lives are not. Understood?"

Chef Brown and Frederick nodded.

Scrumptious Bakery hadn't been open ten minutes before Robin entered fluid with questions. "I heard someone broke into the bakery this morning. My word! What is going on around here? Someone broke into Frank's Hardware store about six months ago. I hope they didn't get away with much, Shianne."

Shianne didn't want to elaborate, but she knew Robin wouldn't settle for "yes" and "no" answers. "Fortunately, they didn't get a lot of money. They took pastries that Frederick was taking to the homeless shelter today. They also took several things from the refrigerators—lobster and deli meat, chicken salad, and other items."

"Now, what will they do with all that food but get fat?"

Her response tickled Shianne, but she restrained herself from laughing. "Maybe they were homeless or starving."

"Were any of your workers here when it happened?"

"No. Nobody was here yet." Shianne balled her fists and pursed her lips. "I'm so furious. I wish I could be in a boxing ring with whoever broke in here. I'd knock them crazy." She exhaled deeply. "I have to do something. I have to fight back. Maybe we should meet with the businesses around here and talk about the uptick in burglaries. I bet Frank is willing. He's still furious about the burglary at his store."

"Not only Frank but all the business owners. I'm on board. So, what's our plan?"

"Well, we can invite Officer Reed, who was here earlier, to our meeting. He can suggest how to beef up surveillance in the area. It's important that everyone feel safe."

Robin pumped her fist in the air. "That's an excellent idea. Let's call a meeting, and I'll have the chamber sponsor it. We can have it at the library or maybe here."

"Um, here?"

"Yes. Here at the bakery. What better place to have it? It's ideal."

Shianne hesitated. "Sure. And we should meet soon, while the burglaries are on everyone's mind."

"Sounds good. We can serve pastries and coffee. Maybe you can make some of those little sandwiches you had at your opening. You know, Bill at the paint store, likes to eat." Robin winked.

"And I'll ask my friends to help post flyers of the meeting around town," Shianne said, her excitement growing.

"Sounds like a plan. I'll post the meeting on our business webpage."

Shianne sighed. "We can't have people afraid to patronize our stores, Robin."

It was after two that afternoon that Shianne got a breather and could return Michelle's and Erica's calls. She three-way called the girls.

"I'm coming over," Michelle shouted upon answering the phone.

"So, am I," Erica echoed and hung up.

Shianne clicked off the phone and leaned against the chair for a quick nap. Twenty minutes later, Michelle rushed into her office, with Erica arriving shortly afterward.

"Are you all right?"

"What time did this happen?"

"Did anyone get hurt?"

"Did they take a lot of money?"

"Why didn't you accept our calls?" the girls asked one after another.

"Ladies, I can only answer one question at a time. Quiet down. Goodness!" She paused. "Sorry, but it has been a day."

"We were concerned about you," Michelle said. "I would have come over had I not been in Chicago. I don't care what Chef Brown told me on the phone."

"Me too," Erica added. "Chef Brown doesn't run things here."

Shianne ran her hands through her hair. "Don't get mad at Chef Brown. I asked him to hold all calls. The phones were ringing off the hook with calls from reporters, businesses, and friends. Everybody and their mother have been calling. I didn't want to talk to anybody. I was at a loss for words. I needed time to process this before I talked with anyone. I hope you understand."

"Sure." Michelle nodded. "But you know it worried us. We wanted to be here for you. I can only imagine what you're feeling."

Erica scrolled through her phone. "Here's an article on the burglary. Burglar Walks off with Dough at Scrumptious Bakery," she read aloud.

Michelle's head perked up. "That's a catchy headline."

"Not now, Michelle," Erica said. "This isn't Marketing 101. It says police are investigating a robbery at the Scrumptious Bakery in downtown Evanston." She read further and then clicked off her phone. "The burglar came through the ceiling?"

Shianne nodded. "Police believe so."

"Man, they were determined. Too bad the person didn't get stuck in the ceiling," Erica said, grinning. "That would have been too funny, their legs dangling in the air while they waited to be rescued."

"I thought they should have fallen and broken their legs," Shianne said, twirling her wedding ring on her finger in nervous frustration. "You should have seen the place! Flour strewed all over the floor, tables and chairs overturned. I don't understand why they trashed the place. Who would do something like that? All they had to do was take what they wanted and go. This is disgusting!" She rubbed the tears welling in her eyes. "Gregory and I hadn't been sleeping long before we received the call from the police. It was date night."

She gestured to Michelle. "How was my baby this morning?"

Michelle smiled. "She was good. I love my Friday mornings with her. I made bear pancakes for breakfast."

Shianne placed her hand over her heart. "And thank you for asking Mama Samantha to keep her tonight. I have to try and clear my head. I'm so upset. I've been cussing all day."

"And rightfully so," Erica interrupted. "I'd be pissed too."

"No problem," Michelle said. "You know Mama will help in a heartbeat. She called me after hearing about the bakery, asking if she could do anything. I asked if she would keep Kaiya tonight so you and Gregory can unwind."

"I love her madly," Shianne said, and then hesitated. "Michelle, I neglected to tell you they took the large container of chicken salad I made yesterday."

"Ah, hell no! Not the chicken salad."

"Yes, the chicken salad, boo."

"Where's my pistol?" Michelle removed a hairbrush from her purse and stepped toward the door. "Point me in the path of the chicken salad bandit."

The girls wailed with laughter.

"I needed that laugh," Shianne said, her bronze skin reddening.

"I'm serious. I'll fight for your chicken salad, girl."

"We don't know if the burglar was a man or woman or both," Shianne said. "They discovered a woman's pink and white hat outside in the back."

"Are they thinking a woman robbed the bakery?" Erica asked.

"It's a possibility. We'll see what the surveillance videotapes show."

"Joking aside, I'm sorry this happened to you," Michelle said. She took Shianne's hand in hers. "You don't deserve this. No one does, for that matter. You've been working so hard to build your business."

"There is one thing that frightens me, though," Shianne said. "The burglar might have snatched a piece of mail from my desk that has our home address on it."

"Oh, I would be worried about that too," Michelle said. "I pray they don't try to break into your house, Shianne."

"So, do I."

Frederick entered the office with scrunched eyebrows. "Mrs. White, Mr. Montgomery, is here. He wants to talk to you."

Shianne waved him away. "Would you please tell Mr. Montgomery I'm unavailable, and I'll talk to him soon?"

"He said he heard about the burglary and wanted to make sure everyone was all right."

"Tell him we're fine and thank him for his concern."

Erica knew by the line forming across Shianne's forehead that she better stay silent.

Frederick left, and the girls eavesdropped.

"Thanks. Tell Shianne I'm glad to hear everything is okay," Miles said.

They continued listening until they heard the door chimes ring, indicating Miles had left the bakery.

Shianne covered her forehead with her palm. "Is he going to be around at my every turn?" She took a few deep breaths and collected herself. "Police said I'm the third burglary in this area in six months. That reminds me, Michelle, would you make a flyer for me? I was chatting with Robin, and we're calling a meeting of the business owners next week. We have to work together to try and stop what's going on around here."

"Sure. When's the meeting?"

"Monday evening. I'm closing the bakery early. I called Officer Reed, and he agreed to meet with us."

"Sure. Sure. I'll do it this evening, and email it over to you."

Erica leaned back in her chair. "I think you should get a gun."

Shianne exhaled a deep sigh. "That's what Gregory said."

"Gregory and I finally agree on something? Incredible."

"I'll apply for a FOID card, but I'm not sure if I want a gun."

"You don't need a large gun. Get a three-eighty or a Beretta," Erica said.

"Is that what you have?" Michelle asked.

"No. I have a nine-millimeter Smith & Wesson and a rifle. I'll blow a sucker away."

"You've got to be kidding," Shianne said, flabbergasted.

"Y'all forgot I spent many of my summer vacations on a farm. Granddaddy taught us how to shoot. He said learning how to shoot a gun was just as important as going to school. People are doing some crazy things out here."

"Like breaking into a bakery and stealing donuts and chicken salad," Michelle said.

"It was unnerving, walking into this place this morning," Shianne said.

"I'm sure it was. So, get a gun," Erica said.

Shianne sighed. "I'll think about it."

"Sooner than later, I hope."

"Well, thanks for coming to see about us. We appreciate it. I'm happy I let you girls be my friends." She opened her arms to hug them both.

Michelle giggled. "Ah, here we go again with that let you be my friend stuff."

"I won't argue with you about it today," Erica said. "But tomorrow's another day."

The girls stayed at the bakery until closing, helping Shianne get things ready for the next business day.

Shianne and Gregory were so tired by the time they got home they went straight to bed. Shianne awoke the following day, feeling full of hope. She dreamt of Grandma Eva standing over her, advising that everything would be all right at Scrumptious Bakery. And before kissing Shianne on the forehead, Grandma Eva had told her to add more pepper to her chicken soup.

CHAPTER FOURTEEN

Bakery

The thirty business. owners attending Shianne's meeting were fired up.

"We have to be on higher alert," Tom, a portly man with a round face, said. "This has to stop."

He gestured to Officer Reed. "Though it's a small number, I'm seeing more homeless people panhandling on Golf Road. Can the police do something to stop this?"

A few dissenting gripes rippled in the air.

"That's several blocks away. Are you saying homeless people are breaking into the stores?" a grey-haired woman asked. "Homeless people come into the library daily, and they aren't criminals. Many have just landed on hard times."

"I'm just saying …"

"Well, let's say I'm not in agreement with you," the woman mumbled.

Robin stood next. "Do you have any ideas on what we can do to make the area safer, Officer Reed? Most of us have surveillance cameras and other security devices. Can we get more patrolling later at night?"

"We have expanded our patrolling in the area," Officer Reed said.

"I wear a lanyard." Bob touched a purple cord around his collar. "It notifies police immediately if I hit the button."

"I have an alarm under my countertop," Tom said.

Patrice, a petite woman and owner of Wits End Candles said, "My store is small, and I don't know if I require much security."

"I'd be happy to come by and examine the options for security," Officer Reed said. He looked around the room. "One thing I noticed while patrolling the area is some businesses could have on a few more lights after hours, And, I'm sure everybody knows this, but should someone try to rob you, give them whatever they want. Don't be foolish. Your life is more important than protecting your stores."

"That's what I told my team," Shianne interjected.

The meeting lasted for more than an hour. Afterward, the group chatted with Officer Reed and amongst themselves before leaving.

Talk of Shianne getting a gun resurfaced as the girls cleaned up from the meeting.

"I've been saying for the longest that you should get a gun," Erica said.

"Me too," Gregory agreed. "Shianne, you must be able to protect yourself."

Shianne turned to Erica. "Unlike you, Stagecoach Mary, I'm not comfortable with a gun."

"Stagecoach Mary?" Michelle repeated. "Who's that?"

"You've never heard of Stagecoach Mary?" Erica asked amused.

Michelle shook her head. "No, I haven't."

"She's a legend," Erica said. "Stagecoach Mary was the first black woman to deliver the mail."

"Hump. She sounds extraordinary. Let me find the sister on the internet." Michelle scrolled through her phone.

"Yes, do that. Look her up under badass, gun-toting Mary Fields," Erica said.

Michelle stopped scrolling. "Here she is." She read aloud, "Mary Fields, born in 1832, died in 1914, was the first African-American female star route mail carrier in the United States." Michelle read to herself for a few moments. "Wow, what a remarkable woman. She was a boss, a true pioneer. She didn't start carrying the mail until after she was sixty years old! The article says she was hired because she hitched a team of six horses faster than anyone applying for the job."

"She was also a successful businesswoman. She owned a laundry and a few restaurants during her lifetime," Shianne said. "She's my hero. Can you imagine a black woman being an entrepreneur during the times of the Wild West?"

"She was phenomenal all right," Michelle said.

"Girlfriend got it in, too," Erica said. "They say she smoked cigars and drank whiskey in the saloons with the men. And, according to legend, she even fought and beat some of the men," she said, grinning.

The three went silent for a moment, reflecting on Mary Fields until Erica pulled her cell from her jacket.

"I know someone who can give you shooting lessons, Shianne. His name is William Tompkins. I can put you in touch with him."

"Okay …"

"Hey, why don't we take the class together?" Michelle said to Shianne. "It could be fun. Let's make it a girl thing if Gregory doesn't mind."

He shook his head. "No, I don't mind, just as long as she learns how to shoot."

"I'll come with," Erica said. She positioned her hands in the air as if she were holding a gun. "I can get in a little practice."

Erica checked her watch. "It's not too late. Let me see if I can reach him now." She walked away from the girls and talked.

Moments later, Erica returned with a broad smile. "William's available next Tuesday evening. Is seven o'clock good for everyone?"

Shianne and Michelle nodded.

"Great! Bring your good eye," Erica said.

Michelle laughed. "I can't wait."

"William is a superb instructor. He'll teach you everything you need to know about guns. And he's giving you the Erica discount. He's also good on the eyes, which means Michelle will pay attention."

Michelle's eyebrows furrowed. "What does being good looking have to do with teaching us how to shoot a gun? If he's so good looking—"

"He's Aaron's cousin."

Shianne threw back her head and laughed. "What does he being Aaron's cousin have to do with anything?"

"There you go again."

"I'm telling the truth."

"Oh, shut up. You ladies just be ready next Tuesday."

CHAPTER FIFTEEN

Bakery

Shianne's stomach churned all day at the thought of gun practice that evening. Had the girls not agreed to go with her, she would have canceled. She tried convincing herself that getting a gun was reasonable, but thoughts of Kaiya getting ahold of the weapon reminded her why she shouldn't.

A few years back, when Kaiya was a toddler, someone had broken into their apartment and stole a TV, jewelry, and other keepsakes. Fortunately, she and Kaiya had been away. Neighbors had urged her to get a gun, but she had been too afraid. She'd read and heard too many horror stories of kids getting ahold of their parents' guns and shooting themselves or someone else. She couldn't live with herself if Kaiya were to get ahold of her gun, nor if she had to shoot someone.

As the time neared for the class, Shianne changed into her shooting gear—a blue jogging suit and tennis shoes—and waited for the girls. They'd planned to meet at Scrumptious and ride to the firing range together.

"Let's get this show on the road," Erica said, stepping into the bakery. "It's shooting time."

Shianne looked at Michelle and then at Erica and said, "Okay Pistol Girl, I'm ready."

Shianne and the girls then said their goodnights to Chef Brown and Frederick and headed to the range.

Shianne's temperature rose as they entered the shooting range. Seeing so many guns; semi-automatic handguns, assault weapons, and shotguns intimidated her.

Michelle approached a gun display and pointed at a pearl-handled gun. "I like this one. It's kind of cute."

Who thinks of a gun as cute? Shianne thought.

"That's a Ruger," a man with deep black eyes and a close-cropped beard said, standing behind her. His appearance unsettled her, being she hadn't noticed him standing behind her.

Erica and Shianne watched the two.

"Hi, I'm William."

Michelle's eyes peaked. "Hey, I'm Michelle."

"Nice meeting you." He shook her hand and gestured for Erica and Shianne to join them. He led the girls into a room. "You might be slightly nervous if this is your first time here," William said, standing in front of them.

"You're putting it mildly," Shianne said.

"It's okay if you feel uneasy, a little afraid if you haven't shot a firearm. You don't know what to expect. I want everybody to relax, take a deep breath, and listen. You'll find it's not as bad as you thought."

"Erica was right," Michelle whispered to Shianne. "He is handsome."

"I told you he was fine," Erica added.

"By the end of this class, you'll know about gun safety, the laws regarding firearms, and how to load, shoot, and unload a weapon," William continued.

Shianne let out a deep sigh. Erica wrapped her arm around her shoulders, but Shianne shivered.

"I can't help it. I'm on pins and needles."

"It'll be okay, you'll see," Erica said. "It'll be as easy as the pies you bake by the time we finish the course."

William overheard the comment. "You'll be fine. Most people are a little anxious their first time shooting."

The women eyed each other and shook their heads.

"Shianne, if you have questions, please ask," William said. "The more questions you ask, the more you'll learn. There's a saying, 'Ask first, then you won't have to apologize later.' Right, Erica?"

"You are so right."

"Okay, let's get started."

He looked at Michelle. "Do you have another shirt you can put on?"

Michelle raised an eyebrow.

"The reason I ask is I don't think your beautiful blouse will protect you should a shell casing hit you. I don't want you getting burned."

Michelle fiddled with the hem of her purple top with its flowing sleeves. "Burned?"

"Yes. A few weeks ago, we were at the range, and a woman was firing a nine-millimeter semi-automatic. With these guns, the shell casings eject, and, when they do, they're hot. A casing went down her sleeve, and she panicked."

Shianne shuddered at the thought. Her eyebrows shot up.

"Can anyone tell me what happened when she panicked?" William asked.

Erica raised her hand.

"Sorry, Erica, but I want one of the other ladies to answer. They aren't as familiar with a firearm as you."

"I can only guess," Shianne said, "but I think when she panicked, she lost control of the gun."

William clapped his hands together, smiling. "You're right. In her panic, she turned around and swept people with the muzzle. People were ducking and scrambling to get out of the way of the gun. I had to grab her hand to steady her. The gun should always point downward or at your target."

He faced Michelle. "So, can you change into another shirt?"

"I have a sweater in my gym bag."

"Perfect."

Erica smiled and whispered, "Gym bag? Since when have you been going to the gym? You mean your Darius overnight bag."

"Same difference."

"We'll give you a few minutes to change, Michelle," William said.

Michelle strutted out of the room and returned moments later, wearing an orange sweater.

"Cute sweater, girl," Erica said. "Hey, that looks like my sweater. How did you get it?"

Michelle put a hand on her hip. "Can we talk about this later? We're here for more important business. You left it in my car anyway. I think it was the night Paul picked you up and you guys went for a so-called 'ride.'"

Erica shrugged.

"What were you doing in my car that you left behind your sweater anyway?" Michelle asked with a glare.

"All right, ladies," William said, smiling. "I hate to interrupt your juicy conversation, but it's time to get started."

The girls quieted and then rented their guns, ammunition, and paper targets.

"Who's going first?" William asked as the girls put on their ear and eye protection.

Michelle stepped backward. "Shianne's going first."

"Me? Why me?" She adjusted her glasses that felt more like goggles, not feeling like they were sitting correctly. "Whatever. I'll go first."

William walked her through how to staple the target onto a cardboard backing. With his help, Shianne then loaded her magazines into the gun, got into position, and slowly fired.

"Whew," she said, feeling the power of the weapon. Her hands trembled.

"Not bad," William said, looking at the target. "Not bad at all. I can't believe this is your first time shooting a gun."

"Yes. Yes, it is," Shianne said with an enormous grin.

"Okay, Ms. Michelle, your turn."

William helped her set up as he had done for Shianne. Michelle fired.

"I think you girls have been pulling my leg," William said, observing her shot.

Erica strutted to her bay, loaded her gun, and hit the mark like a pro.

"Show off," Michelle said.

Erica grinned. "I brought my good eye."

After practice, they went to the lounge to decompress before going home. "Would anybody like something to drink?" William asked.

"I'd like a delicious glass of water with lemon, please," Erica said.

"What about you, ladies?" he asked Michelle and Shianne.

"Sure. Cranberry juice for me," Michelle said. "Thanks."

"Cranberry juice for me also, with a slice of lemon," Shianne added.

She nudged Michelle as William went away. "I think he likes you."

Michelle blushed. "What makes you say that? No, he doesn't."

"Yes, he does," Erica quipped. "Can't you see how he keeps looking at you?"

"No, I can't. I probably looked scared as hell."

"No, that's Shianne."

William returned with a tray bearing their drinks. He set the tray before them, and the girls took their glasses.

"I enjoyed the class today. It was fun. You'll have your certificates in no time," William said.

"Yes!" Shianne said, high-fiving Michelle.

"Next week, same time?" William asked.

"Sure," Shianne said. "This wasn't as bad as I expected."

"I told you," William said, playfully wagging a finger at her.

Moments later, William walked the ladies to Shianne's car. "See you, ladies, next week," he said. "Michelle," he said quieter as she was getting into the car.

She angled to him. "Yes?"

"I was wondering if I could take you to dinner one evening."

She shook her head. "William, I have a boyfriend."

"It's just dinner. We'll have some good food and conversation. That's all."

Michelle squinted. *Didn't this man hear me tell him I have a boyfriend?* "I don't think that's a good idea." She slid into the car and, before closing the door, said, "Goodnight."

"Whew-wee. It looks like William has the hots for Michelle," Erica said.

"Girl, stop," Michelle said, a sour look coming on her face.

"You stop. I'm telling Darius. William will chase you down, girl. He's one of those men who don't accept rejection easily."

Michelle shrugged.

"What did he say to you?" Shianne asked. "You guys were talking so low."

"He asked me to dinner."

"What did you say?" Erica asked.

"What do you think I said?"

"Did you look at the man? Didn't you see how fine he is?" Erica asked, laughing.

She turned to Shianne. "She's lying."

"Just because you date every good-looking man who comes your way..." Michelle countered.

"I do not. And we'll see how this pans out, little Ms. Michelle. Remember, you have a few more classes with William."

"We shall see. If I were you, I wouldn't bet any money on William."

Shianne dropped the ladies off at the bakery to pick up their cars and then drove home. She was so thrilled at how the class had gone and wanted to tell Gregory. She clicked on the phone, and the monitor showed she had a few messages from him.

"Hey, honey, I see you called. Your wife did great at practice today! I practiced with a Colt 1911."

"Wonderful, baby." His voice turned urgent. "They caught the burglars. Officer Reed called me this afternoon."

"They did?" Her heart quickened.

"I'm pulling over. I don't want to be distracted." Shianne pulled into a nearby fast-food restaurant and parked. "Okay, honey, what did he say?"

"Officer Reed said they recognized the suspects from a burglary in January. Police arrested them last night at an apartment not too far from the bakery. They found evidence linking them to the bakery, including your Scrumptious Bakery apron. Can you believe it?" He paused. "They also found a piece of mail that had our home address circled with a black marker."

She went speechless.

"So, two people were involved?" she asked moments later.

"Yes, and one of them was a woman. They believe she's the guy's girlfriend."

"So, the hat belonged to her?"

"I don't know."

"How old were they? Did Officer Reed say?"

"No. He wants to drop by the bakery and brief us."

Shianne leaned against the seat. "All right, honey. Tell Officer Reed to come by the bakery anytime."

"I asked him to come tomorrow afternoon. That way, I'll be there too."

Shianne exhaled a deep sigh. "Okay. I'm on my way home. I'll see you in a few."

Shianne clicked off the phone. A chill came over her. Thoughts of her home targeted by the burglars drew ire. *I'm getting a gun.*

News that police had caught who'd burglarized Scrumptious Bakery moved swiftly among local businesses. Some owners called Shianne expressing their joy, while others visited the bakery for more information.

"I'm so glad they caught the burglars," Robin said as she sipped from her hot caramel latte. "Everyone can breathe a little easier."

"We're ecstatic over here! Chef Brown and Frederick have been whistling all morning," Shianne said.

Robin nodded. "I hope everyone is following Officer Reed's suggestions and making sure their businesses are well lit. But, knowing cheap Pete, he probably isn't, if it involves spending some money."

"Is he that cheap?"

Robin rolled her eyes. "He's cheaper than cheap. Pete will try to sell you a coupon."

Shianne laughed. "Goodness. That is cheap."

CHAPTER SIXTEEN

Bakery

BOOM!

Shianne's hands tightened around the steering wheel as her car inched forward. *What the hell is going on?* She glanced through her rearview mirror and noticed a blue car had crashed into hers. Without thinking, she unstrapped her seatbelt and bolted to the driver's window.

"You hit my car! We're at a red light. Why didn't you stop? What's wrong with you?"

"I'm sorry," the silver-haired man said, rolling down his window. "I was test driving this car, and I didn't know how to stop it." He ran his hand through his mane. "I didn't know how to work the brakes. They didn't show me."

"What? You're telling me you don't know how to use the brakes?" She rolled her eyes in disbelief. "Then you shouldn't be driving. It was irresponsible for you to get behind the wheel, especially with snow on the ground." Within moments, Shianne felt awful for yelling at the senior-looking man.

He exited the car and walked in front of the vehicle to assess the damage. "Your back end doesn't look bad."

Shianne gasped. Even in the nightfall, she could see her car was damaged. "Man, are you crazy? Your car's bumper is resting on my car's bumper. I'm calling the police."

Shianne limped to her car and snatched her cell from the seat. While talking with the dispatcher, the man drove off.

"Oh, no, you don't," Shianne said. She hopped into her car and pursued him, flashing her lights as she drove. The man did not stop.

"Ma'am, are you all right?" the dispatcher asked.

Shianne felt intense pain in her knee but told the dispatcher she was okay. "I'm following him. He got into his car and drove off."

"Ma'am, can you read his license plate number?"

"Yes," Shianne said and read the number to the dispatcher.

"Okay, ma'am. The police are on their way. Find a safe place to park. They'll be there in a few minutes."

Shianne continued to pursue the vehicle.

"Have you pulled over to a safe spot, ma'am?" the dispatcher asked moments later.

"He'll get away," Shianne said and gave the dispatcher the direction the two were driving.

"Ma'am, will you please pull over? It might not be safe for you to follow him. He could hurt someone else or himself by trying to get away from you."

"I know. But I'm tired of people getting away with this." Shianne recalled the numerous hit-and-run stories she had heard on the news or read about in the newspapers.

"I know, ma'am," she said with exasperation in her voice. "But, please pull over."

Shianne followed the man until he pulled into an auto dealership. She parked in an adjacent lot and informed the dispatcher of the location.

Moments later, two police cars arrived. One car stopped at the dealership, while the other car pulled alongside Shianne's car. The officer talked to Shianne about the accident. Within minutes, the second officer approached them. The man sat in the back seat of the police car.

"Ma'am, the gentlemen said you agreed your car wasn't damaged, and that you felt comfortable with him leaving."

"He's lying. He's telling a bare-faced lie. I told him I was calling the police, and he took off. Look at my car. Does it look like everything's okay?" Shianne's heart rate increased, and her body temperature warmed.

"I've arrested him for fleeing the scene. We had calls from two motorists who saw the accident. You can pick up a copy of the accident report at the police department in a few days," the officer said.

Shaking, Shianne looked at the guy and yelled, "Maybe next time you won't flee an accident." The man looked straight ahead, saying nothing. The officer then drove off.

Shianne immediately called Gregory about the accident, and he beat her home minutes later.

"Are you sure you're okay?" he asked, opening her car door.

"My knee hurts. I must have bumped it against the dashboard." She exited the car and could hardly stand for the pain. She groaned and grimaced, leaning on Gregory for support.

Gregory wrapped his arm around her waist. "I'm taking you to the hospital."

"I don't want to go to the hospital."

"You can't stand, Shianne. Look at you."

Gregory helped her into his car and drove to the hospital. The two sat quietly for several moments before Gregory said, "Are you crazy, Shianne?" His voice trembled. "Why did you follow the guy?"

"The man hit my car and sped off. What was I supposed to do?"

"Wait for the police!" He shook his head in disgust. "You put yourself in danger, baby. I can't believe you did that."

Shianne sat quietly, knowing Gregory was fuming. "You're right. I should not have followed him. The police arrested him. I hope he stays in jail."

"Let's make sure you're okay, and I'll follow up with the police department tomorrow."

Shianne nodded, her spirits lifted at Gregory's promise.

"If something had happened to you, would it have been worth following the man?"

Shianne didn't answer.

Gregory ran into the hospital's emergency room and brought out a wheelchair to keep her from walking on her hurt leg. Once inside, the ER doctor ordered several tests and X-rays, which revealed a small meniscus tear in her knee.

"You're to limit your activities, including walking, and ice your knee every three to four hours for a few days, Mrs. White. Also, elevate your knee with a pillow when sitting down. I'll write you a few prescriptions to help with the pain and swelling," the doctor said.

Shianne looked at him as if he were speaking a foreign language. "Doctor, I own a bakery. I can't sit around. I have to go to work. We have several upcoming parties to cater. Thank goodness this didn't happen to me during the Christmas rush."

"If you don't want to further damage your knee, which could call for surgery and longer healing time, my advice is to get off your feet and let the healing process begin."

Shianne bowed her head in sadness.

Gregory rubbed her shoulder. "We'll take care of the bakery, baby. Chef Brown and Frederick know how to run things. Give your knee a few days to heal, and then you can return to work."

"How had you been feeling before the accident, Mrs. White?" the doctor asked.

Shianne looked perplexed, her brows drawing together. "Okay, I guess. I've been a little tired, but that happens with running a bakery and having a family. Is there something wrong?"

The doctor grinned. "You're feeling more fatigued because you're pregnant."

Her eyes enlarged. Her mouth hung open. "Pregnant?" She pressed her hands to her cheeks and glanced at Gregory in disbelief. "You're kidding me, aren't you?"

"No. You're pregnant. It looks like you're a few months along."

Gregory grinned. "We're having a baby?"

"Pregnant. I don't believe this. I can't be pregnant right now. Now is not the time!"

"Babies can be a surprise sometimes," the doctor replied. "They don't always come at the most opportune time."

Shianne's mouth twisted into a wry grin.

"The medicines I've prescribed are safe for you to take with your pregnancy," he said, typing into the computer.

The room quieted for several moments.

"You're having a baby, Shianne. We're having a baby," Gregory said elatedly.

Shianne sat numbly.

"Mrs. White, remember to stay off your feet for a few days and follow up with your doctors about your knee and pregnancy. And congratulations on the baby."

"Thanks," she replied with a deep breath. Had she not opened the bakery, Shianne would be ecstatic about her pregnancy. But with the bakery in full swing, it brought about a bit of anxiety.

Shianne's cell had sounded a few times in the ER, but she couldn't answer it while undergoing testing. She called Michelle back as Gregory wheeled her to the car.

"Are you okay?" Michelle asked as soon as she answered Shianne's call.

"Yes and no. Fortunately, I didn't break anything, but the doctor advised me to stay off my feet for a few days."

"Ah, no. Bummer."

"Yeah, that's what I said. He also dropped a surprise on me, but I'll tell you about that later."

"Don't worry. Everybody will chip in and take care of you and the bakery. Do you need anything?"

"No, we're headed to the pharmacy to fill my prescriptions and then go home."

"Keep your leg elevated. I'll be over tomorrow. And what's this I'm hearing about you chasing the car that hit you? You know better than that. That man could have done anything to you."

"Who told you?"

"I called the house, and the babysitter told me. She must have overheard Gregory talking with you. I don't know."

"That big mouth."

"Perhaps she was frightened at hearing you were in an accident. What does a teen know about discretion?"

"Yeah. Yeah." The pain was irritating Shianne, and she didn't want to talk further. "I'll talk to you tomorrow. Okay?" she said before clicking off her cell.

As he drove home, Gregory glanced at Shianne with a delighted look on his face. He opened his mouth as if he were about to say something, but Shianne got her words out first.

"Gregory, please don't say anything. Please don't."

He shifted his gaze to the road, the look of joy still on his face. "I'm happy you're pregnant. You know I've wanted us to have a child for a long time." He patted her hand. "It'll be okay. We'll get through this as we've done with other things. I'll step it up more."

"I can't believe I'm pregnant."

He smiled. "I don't know why it's such a shock, Shianne. You aren't on birth control, and we've had some great date nights."

Shianne smiled back. "We have. Haven't we."

Shianne was lying in bed, a pillow under her knee, and watching TV when Michelle meandered into her room with flowers.

"Aw, so beautiful," Shianne said. "Thank you."

"I thought they'd cheer you up. How are you?" Michelle asked, putting the flowers on the nightstand.

Shianne nodded. "I'm better than I was last night. The pain was excruciating."

"I'm sure it was. When's the last time you took something for pain?"

"I took some Tylenol a few hours ago."

Michelle sat on the foot of the bed. "Tylenol for a torn meniscus? Is that what the doctor prescribed? Girl, I'd be crying, I need drugs."

Shianne took a deep breath. "I thought he would too, but when a test came back saying I was pregnant ..."

"Pregnant?" Michelle's eyes gleamed.

"That's what I said. A few months pregnant."

The sides of Michelle's mouth curved into a big smile. "Oh my god! I'm going to be an auntie again!"

Michelle stood and danced side to side, arms swinging in the air. "Hey! Hey! Go, Shianne! Go, Shianne! Gregory must be thrilled."

"He's elated. He smiled all the way home from the hospital. I talked to my family this morning, and they're so excited. Raquel is already planning a gender reveal party."

"What? You're only a few months."

"Girl, you know how my family does things. So you and Erica can expect a call from Raquel soon."

Michelle nodded. "It'll be good talking with her."

"Being pregnant is settling in with me now, but I tell you, I was in shock last night."

"I don't know why, especially if you and Gregory are having sex on the regular."

"We are. Man, are we." She laughed. "Gregory attributes my pregnancy to our date nights."

"I told you to have fun, but this is not what I imagined."

Shianne exhaled a deep sigh. "Yesterday was so crazy. First, I get in a car accident and I wind up chasing the man who hit me. Then I go to the emergency room for my knee and I walk out pregnant. That sounds like a movie."

"That is pretty bizarre. Have you told Kaiya?"

"We told her last night before she went to bed. She loves the idea of having a little sister." Shianne grinned. "She volunteered to comb the baby's hair every day."

"Uh-oh. That's scary."

Shianne shook her head. "I can't believe all of this is happening to me during my first year of opening the bakery."

"I know, but sometimes things happen when you least expect them. Don't worry about the bakery; Chef Brown can handle things. He's cooked on ships and at high-end hotels and restaurants. Certainly, he can run your bakery. And, if he needs extra help, I'm available."

Shianne laughed. "No. No. No. Stay away from my bakery. You stick to your greeting cards."

"Thanks for the vote of confidence."

Michelle and Shianne chatted a while before Michelle grabbed her purse to go home. "Now, I don't want to find out you tried sneaking to the bakery," Michelle said.

Shianne smirked. "You know, I thought about it."

"I'm sure you did, Mrs. White. You've never been good at taking directions. I'll tell Gregory to tie you to the bed."

"He wouldn't do that, but he will stand outside the door."

Michelle laughed. "Bye, girl."

CHAPTER SEVENTEEN

Gregory was stacking pastry boxes on the shelves when a customer stepped into the bakery.

"Good afternoon. Can I help you?" Gregory asked, approaching him.

"I bought a banana pound cake here a few weeks ago for my wife, and it was delicious, so I thought I'd come by and get another one. I'd also like to try something else from the bakery." He surveyed the glass displays of pastries.

"Our double-chocolate cream pie is a favorite with a lot of our customers."

"Okay, I'll take one."

Gregory removed a pie from the display and set it inside a box. "Would you like anything else? We have blueberry muffins that just came out of the oven."

"Okay, give me a half dozen," Miles said, smiling.

Gregory returned with the muffins moments later.

"Are you Shianne's husband?"

Gregory smiled. "Yes. You know my wife?"

Miles extended his hand. "Miles Montgomery. Shianne and I are old friends. We went to college together."

Gregory pretended not to know of him and shook his hand. "Nice meeting you."

"Is Shianne here? I'd like to say hello."

"No, she's not here. Is this your first time at the bakery?"

"No, I was here a few weeks ago."

"That's right. You did say you'd bought a cake from here. Funny, Shianne never mentioned you coming into the store. I'd think she'd be excited to see an old college friend."

Miles shrugged. "I don't know, man."

"Did you meet Kaiya when you were here?"

"Kaiya?"

"Our daughter."

Miles looked puzzled and shook his head. "No, I didn't get the chance."

Gregory harrumphed and rang up the order. "That'll be Fifty-six ninety-four."

Miles pulled his wallet from his pants pocket and handed Gregory sixty dollars.

Gregory returned with his change moments later. "Thanks, man, for stopping by."

"Tell Shianne I said hi, will you?"

"Sure. I'll tell her you stopped by."

Miles grabbed the box and left the store. Gregory watched him as he climbed inside his red Mercedes and drove off. The thought of Miles coming to the bakery and Shianne not mentioning it irritated Gregory. It weighed on him the rest of the day.

That night, while lying in bed, he sought an explanation. "Babe, Miles came into the bakery today. He said he'd been there a couple of weeks ago. You never mentioned it."

She lay quiet for a few moments. "I didn't? It must have slipped my mind."

"Your ex-boyfriend, Kaiya's father, comes into the bakery, and it slips your mind?"

"I don't know, Gregory. It was busy that day at the bakery, and I forgot."

"Come on, Shianne. It's not like you see him all the time."

Shianne sighed. "Okay, Gregory. I'm sorry, I didn't tell you. But honestly, it wasn't that big of a deal to me."

"Did it cross your mind that it might matter to me? My wife's ex coming into the bakery? What did you talk about?"

"He talked about his family, and that was pretty much it."

"You didn't say anything about Kaiya?"

She sat upright and turned on the night lamp. "No, I didn't! How do you know I didn't?"

"He said you hadn't."

Shianne fumed. "You asked him about Kaiya?" She fluffed her pillows. "Why?"

Gregory sat upright. "Why not? I didn't say anything in particular. I just asked had he met her when he came into the store."

"I was helping a customer when he came into the bakery. Naturally, we talked for a few moments, having not seen each other for some years. Are you thinking I should have told him about Ki then? What was I supposed to say? 'Enjoy your cake, Miles, and, oh, by the way, you and I have a daughter together'?"

"You're not funny, Shianne. I can do without your sarcasm right now."

"I know it's not funny. But what do you want me to say? I don't want you putting more into this than called. Please don't blow this out of proportion."

"I'm not blowing this out of proportion. I just think you should have told me. All you had to say was Miles came into the bakery today." He paused. "Maybe . . ."

"Maybe what?" she asked. "Would it have been enough for you if I'd mentioned it?"

"Yes, but because you didn't, I'm wondering why you hadn't."

Shianne sat quietly, wondering if Gregory was jealous of her seeing Miles again.

"I have no feelings for him, Gregory, and he has none for me."

"How do you know?"

"Because I know. The man is married."

"Oh, because he's married, you're saying he can't still have feelings for you? People step out of their marriage all the time, and you know it."

"Well, there won't be any tipping going on here."

The two sat quietly until Gregory broke the silence. "I'm sorry. I might have overreacted, but I did get a little jealous. You were in love with the man at one time."

"Miles and I are over. I'm surprised you would even think something like that." She touched his hand with hers. "I treated him like a regular customer. Honey, you erased all the hurt, all the thoughts about him when you came into my life."

Gregory wrapped his arm around her. "Well, do you think you'll tell him about Ki?"

"I don't know, honey. I don't know if I'll ever see Miles again."

"Well, he came to the bakery for a second time. I don't think this is the end of him coming."

She gave him an odd look. "I won't speculate on the future. I'll deal with things as they come."

"I know, but I think the man has a right to know. He's her biological father. You don't want her to find out when she's eighteen that I'm not her biological father."

"She might have to. You're the only father she knows."

"You don't mean that. Kaiya will always be my daughter. Our relationship won't come undone if she finds out the truth."

"The child is five years old. Her learning that Miles is her father might be too much for her to handle now. What happens if Miles wants joint custody of her? This can get complicated."

"Complicated for who, you or Kaiya? She'll be mad at us if we keep this from her."

"Honey, I don't know. I don't know what to do." Shianne turned off the lamp, slumped into the bed, and pulled the covers around her.

Gregory watched her for several moments. "So, I guess this means the conversation is over?"

"No. It means I'm going to sleep. I'm sure this won't be our last time talking about this."

Gregory slumped heavily into the bed. "I want us to do the right thing, baby. I don't want us to be like those television talk shows where children learn the man they thought was their father isn't. The child holds so much resentment."

"Please don't equate us with those crazy talk shows."

"They may be crazy, but it's food for thought."

She snuggled closer to him. "We'll do the right thing."

Gregory lay there thinking while Shianne fell asleep within moments. *I hope I'm not overreacting about this.*

CHAPTER EIGHTEEN

Bakery

Shianne was back at the bakery following two weeks of recuper-
ating at home. She'd anticipated returning after a few days, but
she couldn't get around as quickly as she'd liked. But, of all days, she
and Frederick were without the extra set of hands from Chef Brown,
who had called in sick. Together, she and Frederick hosted a luncheon
for seniors and minded the bakery. She was exhausted by day's end.

"One more hour," Frederick said, checking the clock. "Yes. I can't
wait to get off my feet." Shianne sat in a chair and began rubbing her
knee. "I didn't expect my first day back to be so busy."

As she spoke, a young couple appearing to be in their late twenties
arrived at the bakery hand in hand.

Frederick smiled as they approached a display case. "Ooh. I want
this one." The woman pointed at a lemon meringue tart. "No, I'll have
the caramel tart," she replied just as fast.

The guy grinned and chuckled. "I hear the lobster bisque is delicious here."

Frederick smiled. "Everything's great here."

"I'll have the lobster pot pie," the woman said.

"These dishes come with hot buttered French bread, or our famous
cheddar and chives biscuits," Frederick said.

The woman surveyed the hanging menu. "I'll have the French bread."

"And, I'll have the cheddar biscuits," the man followed.

"Will you be eating here?" Frederick asked.

"Yes," the woman said, and the man handed Frederick his credit card for payment.

"Your order will be ready in a few minutes," Frederick said, returning the man's card seconds later.

The boyish-looking man took the woman's hand and escorted her to a table and sat.

Shianne had watched the couple since they'd entered the bakery. She knew many of her customers but had not seen this couple. She stood from her chair and walked over to them.

"Hello. I'm Shianne White, the bakery's owner."

"Hi. I'm Kyle, and this is my wife, Karen."

"Welcome to Scrumptious Bakery. Is this your first time here?"

The couple nodded. "We've passed here several times," Kyle said, "but we hadn't come in."

"Well, I'm glad you stopped in this evening."

"We were on our way to dinner, and, as we drove by, Karen pointed to the bakery. She talks about this place all the time. She's wanted us to come here for the longest."

"My coworkers bring your pastries to work all the time," Karen said. "They're so delicious. And they're always raving about your savory pies."

Shianne touched her heart with her hand. "Thank you."

"When I heard you had savory pies and sandwiches, I thought I'd bring Kyle here one day."

"We don't eat out much," Kyle said. "I've been laid off from my job for over a year and just returned recently. I got my first paycheck today, so I thought I'd take her to dinner. She's made a lot of sacrifices with me being off. We've depended on her salary for mostly every-thing." He looked at Karen then back at Shianne. "Karen's a first grade school teacher at Meadows Elementary School."

"Wonderful. Well, to celebrate your return to work, everything is on me tonight. I'll have Frederick return your money."

"Oh, that's so generous of you," Kyle said. "Thank you. Thank you very much."

"Enjoy yourselves," Shianne said and walked away.

The couple's situation reminded Shianne of her lean years. Kaiya had been just a toddler, and although Shianne had a full-time job and was catering on the side, it was hard managing the bills from month to month. *Thank God that's over.*

Shianne was reading the bakery's customer reviews the next day and was surprised when she saw a response from Kyle Johnson. She clicked on the comment and read aloud.

"Hands down, Scrumptious Bakery has the best lobster bisque around. My wife and I ate at the bakery last night, and the food and pastries were incredible! I recommend the cheddar and chives biscuits. They will melt in your mouth! My mouth is watering thinking about them. But just as delightful as the food is the owner, Shianne White. What a neat lady. She's so kind-hearted. I look forward to eating there very soon. Thanks, Mrs. White, for the great experience."

Shianne's eyes watered. She called for Frederick, who rushed into her office. "Remember the couple that was here last night?"

He nodded. "The young couple."

"Well, Kyle said some nice things about us on our website. Come read what he said about us."

Frederick stood beside her and read the review. "Wow! That's awesome, Mrs. White."

Shianne leaned back in her armchair and smiled. "It's times like this that make it all worth it. There's nothing like bringing a little joy into someone's life."

A moment later, Shianne received an email from Kyle. It read:

Mrs. White, I've been telling my coworkers about our experience at Scrumptious and how generous you were to my wife and me. My supervisor, Dan, suggested you provide the pastries for our employee luncheon next month. If you so kindly accept, you must make enough for 200 people. I'll be in touch.

Shianne's eyes widened with excitement. She looked at Frederick. "Do you see this?"

"Yes! This is great."

Shianne took a deep breath and responded to the message. *Scrumptious Bakery would love to help cater your company's luncheon.*

She stood from her seat and did a little dance.

Frederick joined in dancing side to side. "Beyoncé is Queen B. You're Queen Scrumptious, Mrs. White!"

As they celebrated, Gregory entered the office, holding an unfolded piece of paper in his hand. He raised an eyebrow. "Good to see your knee is doing better."

"Remember the couple I told you about last night? He wrote a raving review about us, and his company wants us to make the pastries for their employee luncheon next month!"

"Okay," Gregory said, unmoved by her excitement. "We need to talk, Shianne."

His reaction puzzled Shianne. She thought he would be more excited. "What's going on?"

Frederick left the room as Gregory handed her the piece of paper.

"What's this?" Shianne reviewed the sheet. Her heart pumped hard as she scanned the payment statement from the bank. *Oh no! Not now. Damn!* She sat for a moment before speaking.

"I borrowed the money about a month before we opened the bakery, thinking we could use it as a cushion if an emergency occurred.

You know what they say about the survival rate for a new business."

Gregory's arms flung into the air. "I know all about one-third of new businesses close their first year, Shianne. I might even understand why you did it. But why didn't you tell me? Why did you sneak behind my back?"

"I wanted the bakery so bad I decided to do it with or without you."

Though Gregory sat quiet, Shianne could hear his deep breathing.

"You were giving me mixed signals, honey. One day you were in, the next day you're singing another tune. I don't deal that way, and you know it. Either you support me fully or not at all. Your actions were driving me crazy."

He squinted until his eyes became tiny slits. "Can you imagine how I'm feeling, knowing my wife borrowed a large sum of money without telling me? Thirty thousand dollars is a lot of money to borrow, Shianne! I'm amazed the bank even let you take out a loan of that size without me." He paused. "Sure, I messed up with the bar, but we agreed we wouldn't hide anything from each other again. We said we would be straightforward regarding our finances. Remember?"

"I'm sorry, but when you kept changing your mind, I felt as if I were on my own. Some days you made me feel like the bakery was just some pipe dream."

He shot her a quick look. "That was never my intention. I just wanted to ensure our finances were all right."

"But you know there are no guarantees with anything, certainly not with a business. I was willing to take the chance, even if it meant borrowing the money."

Gregory folded his hands.

"I'm not making light of this because I know I've hurt you, but I've been doing a good job of paying the loan down." She held up the statement. "I've already paid fourteen thousand."

"How did you pay it down in such a short period? Business is good, but not that good."

"My sisters loaned me a few grand, and I repaid the rest with money from the bakery."

Silence filled the room.

"We don't have to worry about the loan, Gregory."

He grimaced, and his brows furrowed. "We?"

Her eyes rolled. "Yes, we."

Frederick knocked on the door. "Mrs. White, I need your help."

Shianne checked her watch. The bakery had become an after-school hangout for students. They'd meet in their friend circles, ordering donuts, cupcakes, smoothies, and other delights as they chatted and laughed about the school day's activities.

"I'll be right out," she said through the door.

Gregory stood from the couch, and without saying a word exited the office.

Shianne followed behind him, thinking he would help at the counter, but he left the bakery. Shianne dammed the tears as she approached a group of teens with a broad smile.

CHAPTER NINETEEN

Gregory was in the back of the bakery, cleaning a freezer when he heard Chef Brown and a customer laughing. The conversation continued for several moments.

Gregory wiped his hands and went up front to see who Chef Brown was chattering with. Much to his dismay, it was Miles.

"Greg, this is Miles Montgomery," Chef Brown said excitedly. "He's a football coach at Northwestern."

"Yes, I've met Mr. Montgomery."

"How are you doing, man?" Miles asked.

"I'm doing fine."

"I can't stay away from this place."

I bet you can't. "What can we get you today?" Gregory asked, rushed.

Chef Brown eyed him suspiciously.

"I'm picking up an apple pie and a German chocolate cake for my little girl."

"I have them right here for you, Mr. Montgomery." Chef Brown nodded at the boxes of treats. "That'll be fifty-six thirty-one."

Shianne and Kaiya entered the bakery, and Kaiya ran to Gregory. "I had no cavities, Daddy."

"That's great, baby."

Shianne groaned; the last thing she needed to see was Miles. She and Gregory were hardly talking since he found out about the loan, and to have Miles visit the bakery made her sick to her stomach. She walked over to them, struggling not to show her annoyance. "Hello, Miles. How are you?"

"I'm great. How are you?"

"I'm doing well."

She motioned for Kaiya to come to them. "Kaiya, this is Mr. Montgomery."

She smiled. "Hi."

"You're a pretty little girl. You look like your mother."

"Thank you."

"Come on, baby, do you want to help Daddy make some boxes?" Gregory asked, walking away.

"Nice seeing you, man," Miles said.

"Yeah, you too."

"She's so cute," Miles said to Shianne.

"Thank you."

Shianne noticed Gregory watching them from the corner of her eye.

"I'll bring Kira with me the next time I come to the bakery. She can meet Kaiya too."

"It would be nice seeing her."

Kaiya ran over to Shianne. "Daddy told me to bring you this water."

Miles watched her as she handed Shianne the water. "Ah, you're a lefty, Kaiya. I'm a lefty, too. So is Kira, my little girl."

Small beads of sweat formed on Shianne's forehead. A burst of laughter came from a group of teens approaching the counter. "I guess it's time to get back to work," Shianne said.

"I'll help Chef Brown," Gregory replied. "You and Miles finish talking."

Shianne suspected Gregory's willingness to intervene was to allow her time to discuss Kaiya with Miles. Shianne opened the water and took a drink.

"Miles, can I talk to you for a moment?"

"Sure."

She showed him to a corner table in the rear. "Let's sit here. Would you like something to drink or a piece of pie or something?"

"No, I'm good." He tugged at his shirt.

Shianne took a deep breath. "I don't know where to start, and it might appear I'm babbling, but hear me out. As you know, we had no closure to our break up. We moved on with our lives; you marrying Brandy and me marrying Gregory. Somewhere in-between that time, I had Kaiya, but Gregory isn't the father."

Miles studied her face and shrugged. "It happens this way sometimes. Is her father in her life? If not, I'm sure Gregory is a great father."

"Yes, he's an excellent father to Kaiya, but she's your daughter."

Miles's body stiffened. "Kaiya's my daughter?"

"I didn't know until after we'd broken up that I was pregnant."

He sat back in his chair. "Kaiya's my daughter?" he repeated. "Why didn't you tell me? Why didn't you reach out to me?"

She shrugged. "I was angry. I wanted nothing to do with you then. You'd cheated on me with Brandy, and, when I thought about telling you, I had heard you were engaged."

Miles exhaled a deep sigh. "Kaiya is my daughter. Wow." He gave a puzzled stare. "Shianne, I'm sorry. I didn't expect things to turn out the way they did between Brandy and me. You knew I was just trying to be a part of Kira's life. I never meant to hurt you. I loved you. Still …"

"You didn't love me enough to keep from cheating on me, from sleeping with her, from marrying her," Shianne said, her voice cracking.

"Yes, I cheated on you, but I didn't set out to do it."

"You may have started out wanting to see Kira, but you landed in Brandy's bed."

Miles's body jerked. "If I recall, you upped and moved away. You left without saying a word. I went to your apartment, and you were gone. You didn't tell me where you were going. You left no forwarding address, and your family wouldn't tell me either. That's why I married her. You had hurt me."

Shianne's eyes narrowed. "Hurt you? Do you hear how ridiculous you sound, Miles? And what made you think my family would talk to you? They knew you had betrayed me. What were they supposed to say? You can find Shianne at such and such place? You know Raquel wouldn't tell you."

He frowned. "Raquel didn't like me anyway."

Shianne shrugged. "No, she liked you. It's just once she heard you had cheated on me, she didn't like you."

"She cussed me out and told me not to call her house again," Miles said.

Shianne cocked her head. "And? Do you blame her? I'm her sister, for Christ's sake!" Shianne wanted to laugh but refrained.

They sat silent for several moments.

"I moved away because I was through with you," Shianne said. "I know Brandy's deceased, but I'm sure she wouldn't enjoy hearing that you married her because we had broken up."

"That's not exactly what I mean. After you left, I kept seeing her, and we got married." Miles ran his hand over his face, still processing the news. "This feels like deja vu, first with Kira, now with Kaiya. I wasn't in Kira's life at birth, and now I learn I wasn't in Kaiya's."

"You have to resolve this within yourself. You have to figure out why these things have happened to you. Take a look at what you're doing."

"So, what do we do? How do I make this right?"

"We don't have to do anything. We can continue as is. Gregory has raised her since she was three. He's the only father she knows. I hate messing up her head with our BS."

"You don't mean this; otherwise, you would not have told me. We don't want her growing up resenting both of us, because I guarantee you, she'll find out sometime." He hesitated. "Kira will love having a little sister."

"Maybe so. But, with all respect, this has nothing to do with Kira gaining a sister. As you stated, I don't want Kaiya hating me down the line. However, I don't want to tell her right away, because I believe the timing is everything."

The teens' uproarious laughter disrupted Shianne's thoughts for a moment.

"When I feel she's mature enough to understand the dynamics of all this, I'll tell her," she added with piercing eyes.

"I remember Brandy told Kira about me at about the same age. And things worked out fine for us."

"I'm not Brandy, and Kaiya is not Kira."

Miles's face contorted. "Well, would it be okay if I came by the bakery from time to time and bring Kira?"

"Sure, as long as you say nothing about being her father. And, when I do decide to tell her, I'll talk about what led up to our situation."

A slight frown crept on his face. "Well, I believe in taking care of my responsibilities, so I'll send you money every month to use at your discretion—clothes, college savings account, dolls, whatever. I'll also contact my lawyer to add her to my will."

Shianne said nothing. His offering of financial support made no difference to her.

He shook his head. "This is unbelievable. Shianne, had I not come into the bakery, would you have reached out to me?"

She straightened in her seat. "Maybe, at some point, I would have. I'm telling you now because my husband thinks it's a wise thing to do."

"I don't get you. You despised me so much you couldn't tell me you were pregnant with my child?"

"I did."

His voice softened. "Regardless of how things were between us, we were in a relationship. You knew me. I'm not a monster, and you know that. Sure, I made a mistake, but you knew my heart."

Gregory approached the table and placed a salad before her. "Would you like something to eat, man?"

"Nah, thanks. I'm taking off. I have enough to chew on."

"I have to make sure my baby eats. She gets so busy here she sometimes doesn't eat," Gregory said, smiling. "She told you she was pregnant?"

"Uh, no. Congratulations to you both."

"Thank you," Shianne said.

Miles stood from the table. "I'll be in touch, Shianne." He extended his hand to Gregory. "Thanks, man, for everything."

Gregory nodded and sat beside Shianne. "How did it go?"

"As well as expected, I guess. I told Miles I'd tell her when I felt she was mature enough to handle it. I didn't ask him for anything, but he said he would help support her financially."

"Well, we know it's not about the money."

She exhaled deeply. "I'm glad this is over." Shianne leaned back against her chair and closed her eyes.

"You did the right thing, baby."

Shianne blew air out of her mouth. "I'm a little tired. Will you help Chef Brown close the store?"

"Sure, baby. Go home, and put your feet up. Leave Ki here with me." He kissed her on the forehead. "I'll see you at home."

"This is a surprise," Michelle said, swinging open the door in her silver and white pajamas. "Is the bakery closed?"

"No, the guys are there," Shianne said, walking inside.

"Can I get you something?"

"No." She followed Michelle downstairs to her office and plopped into a chair.

"What goes on? Why the sad face?" Michelle asked, sitting at her desk.

"Miles came by the bakery today."

"Again?"

She nodded. "Again."

"Talk about timing."

"I told him about Kaiya."

Michelle's forehead crinkled. "You did? What made you tell him?"

"I figured now was as good a time as any."

"How did it go?"

"Better than I thought it would. I think Miles left a little bitter, but oh, well. He pissed me off a few times, but I kept my poise. Can you believe he blamed my moving away as the reason for him marrying Brandy?"

Michelle gasped. "Man, get out of here with that mess. No, Miles, you guys broke up because you were cheating on her. You were foul. Your shit was raggedy!"

Shianne straightened. "Miles said he had no plans of getting back together with Brandy because he loved me." She leaned in closer. "And then he said, 'Still.'"

"Still what?"

She shrugged. "I don't know. Miles didn't finish the sentence. He said he'd loved me and still ..."

"What did you say?"

"I didn't say anything." She waved her hand in the air. "It was probably a slip of the tongue."

"Do you think Miles is happy?"

"He appears to be, based on our conversations. He's picking up pastries for his wife and Kira." Shianne recalled how well he had treated her before his indiscretion with Brandy. He had showered her with gifts, taken her away on weekends, and wined and dined her. "But I don't know. He could be crying inside, but that's not my problem."

She paused. "Gregory told him I was pregnant."

"Boy, you guys left no stone unturned this afternoon."

"It was an interesting conversation. No doubt."

Silence filled the room for moments.

"What else is going on?" Michelle asked.

Shianne leaned back in her chair and gazed into Michelle's eyes. "Gregory found out about the loan. He got ahold of the bank statement while I was away from the bakery. Funny thing, it was dated three weeks ago. He didn't question me about the loan until a few days ago."

Michelle's mouth opened wide. "That's odd. Why did he wait so long to ask you about it?"

Shianne shook her head. "I don't know. Gregory can keep things hidden inside for weeks before he finally lets it out. He hasn't said too much to me the past few days, but today, he was gentle."

"Girl, do you need a drink?" Michelle asked sarcastically. "No, I need Jesus to intervene and make things right!"

"This is our prayer," Michelle said. "Amen!"

When Shianne got home later that evening, Gregory and Kaiya had set the dining room table and were waiting for her.

"Kaiya," Shianne called out.

"I'm in here, Mommy."

Shianne entered the room and saw them seated. "Wow, what's this?"

"Kaiya thought we should have something fun to eat tonight," Gregory said, eyeing the spread.

"Right, Mommy," Kaiya chimed in. "We made your favorite."

Shianne gazed at the fish tacos and smiled. "Are fish tacos my favorite or yours, Ki?"

Kaiya grinned as Gregory rose and pulled back the chair for Shianne to sit.

"Thank you guys so much." She turned to Gregory. "I'm sorry."

"We're good, baby. I'm sorry too."

Shianne opened her mouth to speak, but Gregory interrupted her. "Dig in. We can talk later." He handed her the platter of tacos.

Shianne removed two tacos from the plate. "You guys made them just how I like, with coleslaw, avocado, and fresh salsa."

"I helped Daddy make the salsa."

"Ooh, no wonder it looks so good." Shianne bit into the taco. "Yum, this is so delicious, Ki."

Kaiya grabbed a taco from her plate and bit in. She monopolized the dinner conversation, continuing to press her parents for a puppy.

Later that night, while lying in bed, Shianne renewed the discussion about the loan. "Gregory, I'm sorry. I was wrong. But why didn't you talk to me about this earlier?"

"I should have said something the moment I got the statement from the bank. And I shouldn't have acted so stubbornly. Not speaking to you tore me up inside. And you know, not sleeping with you was miserable."

"You made that decision, Gregory. I never, nor will I ever, tell you to sleep in another room."

He snuggled up against her and said, "I missed you."

"I missed us."

Gregory song Michelle Bell's "Make it Like It Was," bringing a broad smile to Shianne's face.

"Man, you're crazy."

"Yes, I'm crazy about you."

CHAPTER TWENTY

It had been raining the proverbial cats and dogs all day. Shianne and Frederick were cleaning the bakery for the night when they heard knocking at the door. Frederick went to the door and opened it.

Erica rushed inside, her umbrella dripping wet from the rain.

"Girl, what are you doing out in this rain?" Shianne asked, stepping into the room. "It's thundering and lightning outside."

"I know, Shianne. I was out in it."

Shianne cocked her head to the side. She knew Erica was not one to stop by unannounced, especially in bad weather. "Come on back. Frederick and I were finishing up."

Erica checked her watch. "I didn't know it was this late." She took a deep breath. "You have any coffee made?"

Shianne poured her a cup and handed it to her. "Let's go to my office. What's going on? You never come here without calling."

Erica followed Shianne to her office and sat on the couch. "I was at the pharmacy getting a pregnancy test."

Shianne gasped and sat next to her. "A pregnancy test? Are you pregnant?"

"I don't know. That's why I got a test. I've missed my period again."

"So, you and Aaron might be with baby?"

Erica shook her head.

"No. Paul and I might be with baby."

Shianne gave Erica a side-eyed glance. "You and Paul?"

"Yes, me and Paul."

Shianne straightened in her seat. "Erica, what have you done?"

"I didn't tell you guys, but I visited him for a few days after Thanksgiving."

Shianne slapped her thighs with her hand. "Ah-ha! You went to Portland, after all. Michelle and I figured you went because every time we called, you'd say you would call us back, but you never did."

Erica gave a sheepish grin.

"So, what if you're pregnant by Paul? How do you know it's Paul's anyway?"

"I know."

Shianne leaned in closer. "How do you know?"

"Because Aaron and I are not having sex."

Shianne's eyes widened. "You're not?"

"We've never had sex."

"Why not? I mean, I assumed you guys were all in the sheets." She clasped her hands in the back of her head and looked at the ceiling. "Suppose you are pregnant? You know this is going to cause some problems for you and Aaron."

"Duh! You think?"

"Does Paul know?"

"Yes." Erica dabbed at the tears spilling from her eyes.

Shianne wrapped her arm around her.

"I haven't had my cycle in two months. It's like clockwork. It screams out the date."

The two sat silent. Shianne eyed the drugstore bag lying beside Erica. "Is the kit inside the bag?"

"Yeah. I'll take the test when I get home."

"Do it here." Shianne gently rubbed her back. "We'll know the results in a few minutes."

Erica clutched her bag, entered the bathroom, and closed the door.

Shianne rested on the couch, unconsciously tapping a foot and picking at a cuticle. Before she knew it, several minutes had passed.

Wondering what was taking Erica so long, she called out, "Erica?"

Erica didn't answer.

"Oh, Erica, old buddy, my friend."

Hearing no answer, Shianne knocked on the bathroom door. "Knock, knock. Are you okay in there? Do you need aid and assist? I'm coming in."

Shianne slowly opened the door.

Erica stood in front of the mirror, crying. Shianne didn't know what to think or say; she wondered if Erica was happy or unhappy with the result. Shianne stepped beside Erica. "Are you pregnant?"

"No," Erica said, holding up the test strip.

"Were you hoping you were pregnant?"

"Somewhat. I know it's crazy, but I liked the thought of Paul and me having a baby."

"Even though you're with Aaron? I thought you were in love with Aaron?"

"Shianne, I'm in love with two men. I love Aaron, but I'm still in love with Paul. As crazy as things have been for us, I've never stopped loving him. I know I've pretended that I no longer cared for him but I do immensely. I always left the door open for Paul and me."

"You're in a hell of a dilemma, girl."

"I wonder why I haven't had my period."

"You should go to the doctor. Take another test."

"I will because my period is always on time." She wiped her eyes. "I guess I'll call Paul on my way home."

"Will you tell Aaron?"

Erica put the kit into the bag. "I don't know." The two left the bathroom.

"Well, go to the doctor and see what's going on with you. If you're not pregnant, you certainly want to find out what's going on with your body."

"Yes, for sure."

Shianne hugged her. "I just took an apple pie out of the oven for dinner tonight. I promised Ki I would make her one. Would you like a slice or two?"

Erica shook her head.

"Aw, come on. You know you love apple pie."

A modest smile inched across Erica's lips. "Sure. You know I can't say no to your apple pie."

Shianne and Erica went into the bakery, where Shianne sliced two pieces of pie and put them in a box.

"There's nothing like a slice of pie when your thoughts are all over the place," Shianne said, handing her the box.

"Thanks for being here for me," Erica said, hugging her.

"You don't have to thank me. That's what we do. You know that."

Shianne walked with her to the door. Erica opened her umbrella and ran to her car.

What has she gotten herself into this time? Shianne thought as she watched Erica get inside her car.

CHAPTER TWENTY-ONE

Bakery

Michelle and Darius had returned to their hotel room following a morning of sightseeing, shopping, and lunch at a quaint outdoor restaurant. When Darius had suggested they take a short trip to Canada for the International Bridge Walk—the 2.8-mile bridge connecting Sault St. Marie, Michigan with Sault St. Marie, Ontario, Canada— Michelle wasn't too excited. Her thoughts of a Canada trip with Darius were more romantic, but traversing the bridge on foot that June weekend with thousands of others was more fun than she'd imagined. They'd chummed with other couples and enjoyed spectacular views of the twin Sault St. Maries, the St. Mary's River rapids, and the Soo Locks.

"I'm having such a good time," Michelle said, stretching out on the couch.

Darius handed her a glass of lemonade and sat beside her. "I knew you would. Canada's a nice place to visit."

His cell rang. Darius sat upright and answered. "Yes, this is he. Uh-huh." He listened intently as the caller spoke. "Thank you for calling."

He placed his phone on the end table. "That was St. Luke's Hospital. Carolyn's had the baby. It's a boy."

Michelle's heart raced. She knew the time would come for Carolyn to give birth, but it had come too soon, and at the wrong time. She and Darius were enjoying their first trip out of the country together. So much so that they planned to extend their stay a few days.

She sat up alongside him, her body temperature rising. "Do you want to leave today?"

He leaned against the couch. "The hospital said the baby is fine. We can leave tomorrow."

Darius took hold of her hand and held it against his heart. She snuggled closer to him. "We knew this day would come, Darius."

He nodded. A smile crept on his face. "I wish it were you having my child instead of her."

Michelle had thought the same. Several times. "Maybe one day."

His grin grew wider. "Carolyn named him after me."

Michelle forced another smile. "I figured she would."

He squeezed her hand tighter. "I love you."

"Love you too." She kissed him on the lips. "Are you going to call Carolyn?"

Darius rubbed his hand across his head. "I don't know. What would I say? I can tell her I'm coming to see the baby tomorrow, and that I'm glad they're both all right. Other than that …"

The two sat quietly for several moments.

Seeing they would leave the next day, Michelle and Darius then discussed how they would spend the remainder of their trip. Plans included more sightseeing, dinner, and dancing that evening.

"Well, let's get dressed," Michelle said, sauntering into the bathroom. While showering, thoughts of Carolyn giving birth permeated her mind. Tears fell down her face. *Father God, give me strength.*

After showering, Michelle put on a pink backless sundress and matching sandals, getting just the reaction she'd hoped from Darius.

"Wow! You look beautiful," he said as she sashayed into the room. "I'll be the envy of every man tonight."

Michelle smiled. "Thank you, baby."

Michelle and Darius had worked up an appetite following sightseeing. They settled at a cozy restaurant and dined on lobster and other dishes. To his surprise, Darius ran into a fraternity brother who was celebrating his birthday with friends. He and Michelle joined the group, and by midnight, they were drinking tequila shots, and Michelle was feeling no pain. The party didn't end until well after 2 a.m. At least, that's the last time Michelle looked at her watch.

Michelle and Darius awakened that morning and had breakfast before bussing from the hotel to Lake Superior State University in Michigan, where the walk had begun and where Darius had left his car. Considering Michelle had a headache, the ride home was pleasurable. She didn't know if the pain in the middle of her forehead was from drinking tequila shots or Darius coming home to a baby.

Michelle sat, staring at the blank computer screen. She was working on a new greeting card, but her mind wouldn't stay focused. Her thoughts were all over the place. She grabbed her cell from the desk and called Shianne.

"Hey!" Shianne said. "Are you home? How was Canada?"

"We had a wonderful time. It was so much fun."

"I bet. I thought you guys were staying longer."

"We were, but Carolyn had the baby, so we came home today."

"She had the baby?" Shianne's voice rose. "Yeah, that would change things. How's the baby?"

"Baby Darius is fine."

"She named the baby after Darius?"

"Yeah, what a shock," Michelle said sarcastically.

"Have you guys seen the baby?"

"Darius is at the hospital now," Michelle murmured. "I hope she doesn't play games with Darius over the baby?"

"Girl, now you know Darius will not let her pull his strings. You don't have to worry about that. Carolyn may have his child, but you have his heart. I know this situation causes stomach upset, but you'll get through it."

Michelle became angry at herself, embarrassed by her selfishness and inability to focus on Darius or his newborn child. "I guess you're right."

"I know I'm right. Just wait, you'll fall in love with the little guy. This baby didn't ask to be here. His parents might have made a mistake, but he's no mistake."

"Exactly, and that's what concerns me. His parents made a mistake. I don't want Carolyn dangling the baby like a carrot."

"Michelle, I don't know how many times I have to tell you the man loves you. He's crazy about you. I see it in his eyes. He told you he didn't want her."

"I know."

"Then believe him, Michelle. Get over it."

Michelle knew Shianne was right, but she wasn't ready to accept it all the way. "So what's going on your way?" Michelle asked, changing the subject.

"Well, I have some good news. Gregory has a job! The company called and offered him the position this morning."

"That's great! Fantastic!"

"Gregory is so happy. He's been dancing around the house for the last hour. Ki and I are dancing too. You should see us!"

"I can only imagine. I'm happy for you guys. When does he start working?"

"In two weeks. The position is similar to his old job, but Gregory will be making more money."

Michelle let out a squeal. "Tell him I said congrats!"

"I was thinking of throwing him a little celebration party Saturday night. I know it's short notice, but I hope you and Darius can come. Erica's already said yes. So have Chef Brown and Frederick."

"I'll come for sure. I have to check and see what Darius is doing."

Shianne chuckled. "Girl, he's doing you. It's on Saturday night, and where is Darius on Saturday nights? With you. You're either at his place or yours."

"Okay, we'll be there. Can I help with anything?"

"No, I have everything I need. I'm thinking about an appetizer-only dinner party. You know, finger sandwiches, cheesy appetizers, dips, and fancy drinks."

"Fancy drinks? It sounds like fun. Remind me to tell you about last night and our fancy drinks."

"Ooh, tell me. Tell me now."

"No, it'll give us something to talk about later," Michelle said, smiling.

"Okay, I'll talk with you later. Night, sweetie."

Michelle clicked off the phone and continued working. Her mood brightened when she opened an email from a business owner wishing to add Michelle's card line in her store. She'd test-marketed Michelle's cards and said her customers loved them.

"Now that's what I'm talking about!" Michelle pumped her arms in the air. "Yes!"

Michelle had sunk into the couch and was near asleep when Darius rang the doorbell, pizza in hand.

"Hey," he said, entering the house and kissing her on the cheek.

"Hey. How did everything go?" Michelle asked, walking back to the living room.

"Things went okay." He placed the pizza on the table and sat next to her on the couch. "He's so cute." Darius's voice was bubbly as he spoke. "I told Carolyn I would keep him anytime she wanted me to.

She said it might be sooner than later."

"I'm sure she did." Michelle pinched herself. She wanted to speak only positive thoughts. "I can help you with Darius if you want me to."

He gave her a puzzled stare. "Why wouldn't I?"

Michelle hunched her shoulders.

"I want you in every aspect of my life, Michelle." He wrapped his arm around her. "Whatever doubts you have floating in that beautiful head of yours, you need to get rid of now, Michelle. It's you and me all the way."

Michelle smiled and rested on him. "That's what I was hoping you would say." She then straightened. "I talked with Shianne earlier and she said Gregory has a job! She's having a dinner party for him Saturday night. Do you want to go?"

Darius smiled as he opened the pizza carton. "Of course, I want to go. That's great news. He was worried job offers weren't happening fast enough. I'd given him a few leads. I wonder if any of them panned out for him." Darius bit into the pizza. "Whatever worked, I'm happy for him."

CHAPTER TWENTY-TWO

Bakery

"Hey, hey, the gang's all here," Erica said, stepping into the house, grinning.

"Why are you late? Everyone's been here for better than an hour," Shianne said, taking the bottle of champagne from her and placing it on a near table.

"I'll tell you later."

Erica exchanged hellos with Gregory as she entered the room. "Congratulations, Gregory! I hear your little vacation is over."

"Yes, but it's okay. I enjoyed helping at the bakery, but I'm ready to get back to work."

"Well, I wish you well, my friend," Erica said. "You certainly deserve it."

"Thanks, he said smiling.

Shianne then moseyed through the house. Chef Brown and Darius had settled into a highly competitive game of chess in the family room while Frederick and his girlfriend, Trenity, a cute twenty-something, filed through CDs as if they were the evening's designated DJs. Erica greeted them and joked with Frederick before going into the kitchen, where Shianne was making a second batch of her special punch.

"Girl, you know how to throw a party," Erica said, scanning the spread of food on the table. Displayed on a white linen tablecloth with copper serving knives were mini quiches, bruschetta, creamy shrimp and kale artichoke dip, cucumber rounds garnished with salmon, chicken wings, meatballs, and pastries of every kind and flavor. Erica reached for a glass garnished with fruit slices and lifted it in the air. "Cheers."

"So, what's going on?" Shianne asked. "Where's Aaron?"

"He's not coming."

"Who's not coming?" Michelle asked, entering the room and over-hearing their conversation.

"Aaron," Erica said.

"I was wondering …"

"We got into an argument if that's what you want to call it." She exhaled. "I told him I still had feelings for Paul."

"What prompted that conversation?" Shianne asked.

"He said I hadn't been acting myself for a while, and that I appeared distant."

"Were you?" Michelle asked.

"I didn't think so."

"Did you tell him about the pregnancy scare?" Shianne asked.

"No, but I slipped and called him 'Paul' today."

"Ouch!" Michelle said.

"That's when we got into this big discussion about Paul. I told him everything."

Michelle inched forward. "Everything?"

Erica grimaced. "Mostly everything. He asked if I'd been lying about my feelings for him. I told him no."

"So, how did you guys leave things?" Michelle asked.

"He broke up with me. He said he didn't want anything else to do with me."

"Are you okay?" Shianne asked.

"No, I'm not okay, but it is what it is. I couldn't promise Aaron that I wouldn't speak to Paul again. I couldn't do that. I won't lie about us."

The girls stood silent for a few moments, digesting the conversation.

"Well," Shianne said eventually. "I guess you've freed your heart for Paul to resurface."

Gregory, Darius, and Chef Brown entered the kitchen, chuckling about the chess game.

"Here you ladies are," Gregory said.

"I was making another pitcher of punch," Shianne said.

Darius wrapped his arm around Michelle's waist from behind. "Chef Brown was quite a challenge. He beat me, babe."

"You play well, man," Chef Brown said. "Good match." He popped a cucumber round into his mouth.

"So, tell me about this job, Gregory," Erica said.

The group listened as Gregory eagerly expounded on his new position. "And I'm making twenty grand more than my last job."

"My man," Darius said, high-fiving him.

Shianne gleamed with joy. "I know I've said this already, honey, but I am so proud of you. I knew you'd bounce back and better than before." She kissed him and lifted her glass of sparkling cider into the air.

"Cheers to Gregory, my fabulous husband."

"Cheers," the group roared.

CHAPTER TWENTY-THREE

Michelle awoke the next morning in good spirits. She showered, put on a pair of jeans and a blouse, and went to the store to pick up a few things. She'd had a taste for spaghetti the past few days and figured she would make a pot while she and Darius babysat little Darius.

While shopping for hamburger, Michelle got a sense someone was watching her. Out of the corner of her eye, she saw a man standing a few feet away, taking in her moves. It was William. *Damn, just what I need.*

William smiled as he approached her. "Good morning, Michelle. How are you?"

Michelle faked a grin. "I'm doing fine. And you?"

"Good. I'm doing a little shopping before I head to the range." He paused. "I still haven't gotten that call from you."

"I don't know what made you think I would call you. I've told you a few times what was up."

He switched the carton of eggs he had been holding in one hand to the other. "That's right; you've said you have a boyfriend." He leaned in closer. "Is the boyfriend still around?"

Michelle smiled. "Yes, he is. I'm making him spaghetti today." She gestured toward her grocery cart containing a bag of onions, spaghetti sauce, and other items. "It's a good day for spaghetti, with the rain and all."

He stared at her as if a thought had shot through his mind. "I bet your spaghetti isn't as good as mine."

Michelle felt he was baiting her. "Maybe not, but it's good."

"Will you save some for me?"

Boy, this guy doesn't stop. "The boyfriend likes to eat, and I'm sure he'll zip through this."

"No worries. I'll save you some of mine."

She shook her head. "Thanks, but you don't have to."

He stared into her eyes. "Well, have a good day making spaghetti for the boyfriend."

"Nice running into you, William." She took hold of the cart and steered it in the opposite direction.

"My dinner invitation remains," he said as she pushed away.

Michelle arrived at Darius's an hour later with sacks in tow. "I thought I'd make spaghetti while we babysit."

He took the bags from her and headed toward the kitchen. "Sounds great."

Michelle glanced at the large white stone clock on the wall. It was 11:30 a.m. Baby Darius would be arriving in thirty minutes.

"We need a nickname for Darius," she said, helping him remove items from the bag.

"Let's call him DJ for Darius Junior."

Her nose wrinkled. "That's very creative."

"Well, do you have a better name?"

"No."

"Then, it's DJ."

Darius appeared restless as she cooked. He constantly checked his watch.

"Are you nervous about keeping him?"

He nodded. "A bit. I've never taken care of a baby. I've just held them for a few minutes and then gave them back to their mamas." He smiled. "I'm glad you're here with me."

"It'll be a piece of cake. Remember, you helped your mom with your brothers."

"Yeah, but they weren't babies."

She wrapped her arm around his shoulders and held him. "You'll be fine. And I'm letting you change all the stinky diapers."

"That's what I was counting on you doing."

"Nope. Sorry."

"Ah, baby, I thought you had my back."

"I do. I'll pass you the wipes." Michelle withdrew a knife from its holder and chopped an onion.

The doorbell rang, interrupting their conversation.

His eyes widened. "That must be them." Darius rubbed his hands together in front of his chest and went to answer the door.

Michelle continued cooking and went into the living room several minutes later. She was surprised Carolyn was still there.

"Hey," Michelle said.

Carolyn looked just as stunned at seeing Michelle. "Hi, Michelle."

Michelle sat next to Darius. "Aw, he's so cute." Michelle had seen pictures of the baby on Darius's phone, but this was her first time seeing him face-to-face. She turned to Carolyn, who was grinning. "How are you doing? You look great."

"Thank you."

"Don't worry about all the weight you've gained. It'll come off in no time." Michelle knew she was insulting Carolyn, but she didn't care.

Darius looked up from DJ and at her.

"Well, let me get out of here. I should be back by five. I'm meeting my girlfriends for lunch and shopping."

"Have a good time," Michelle said.

Carolyn looked as if she was waiting for Darius to escort her to the door. Instead, Michelle rose from the couch. "I'll show you out."

Carolyn grabbed her purse and wordlessly followed Michelle to the door.

"Have a good time," Michelle said again, and quickly closed the door. She grinned to herself before joining Darius in the living room.

Darius eyed her suspiciously. "Was the weight thing a jab?"

"No. No, baby. Did it sound like one?"

"Yes, it did, Michelle."

Michelle grinned. "Well, I'm sorry, because I didn't mean for it to be."

Time passed rapidly with the feeding, changing, and playing with DJ. Carolyn was ringing the doorbell before they knew it.

"I believe that's your mom, little man. It's time to go home. Daddy will see you soon."

"It was nice meeting you, little D." Michelle kissed his hand. Michelle watched Darius as he left the room to answer the door, thinking he'd be a great father for their child.

Carolyn gave Michelle a cool look when she entered the living room.

Why the scowling face? Oh yeah, you met with the girlfriends. They probably dogged me at lunch.

Darius put DJ in the car seat and draped a blanket on him.

"Thanks for keeping him."

"Call us whenever you need a break," Michelle interjected.

Carolyn ignored her.

"I'll carry him to the car," Darius said.

Michelle followed behind and stood at the door as Darius snapped DJ's car seat into the back seat base. He and Carolyn talked for several moments before Darius ran inside.

"What were you guys talking about?"

He took Michelle's hand and led her into the living room and sat. "She said she didn't want DJ around you, and that she'd keep him away from me if you were going to be around."

"Are you serious?"

"I nipped that in the bud right away. I told her I would take her to court if I had to. She's not stopping me from seeing my child. That's ridiculous!"

Michelle swallowed. "So, I guess this is how it will be every time Darius comes around?"

"I told her she has to respect you because we were getting married."

Michelle's eyes widened. "Married? Why did you tell her that?"

"Wishful thinking, I guess."

Silence filled the room, and then Michelle said, "You want to get married?"

"Yes, if you'll have me."

"Is this your way of asking me to marry you?"

"No. . . but if it works," he said, smiling.

Darius reached into his pants pocket, got on bended knee, and removed a small velvet case. A sparkling one-carat diamond ring set inside. He held it before her.

Michelle's heart beat fast. Her eyes gleamed.

"Michelle Taylor Anthony, I know we haven't been together as long as you would like before I asked you to marry me. But, I don't have to wait for years to know I love you, and that I want to spend the rest of my life with you. Will you marry me?"

Her heart skipped several beats as her eyes welled with tears. "Yes, I'll marry you. Yes!" Michelle kissed him.

Moments later, Michelle loosened her arms from around him and sprung from the couch. "I have to call my parents. I have to call Mama. She'll be so thrilled."

Michelle removed her cell from her purse and dialed. "Ma, I'm getting married," she said as soon as Mrs. Anthony answered. "Darius just asked me to marry him!"

Mrs. Anthony let out such a loud squeal that Darius heard her response a few feet away. He smiled.

"Ooh, I have to call your father. He's getting the tires changed on the car."

"He gave me his blessing," Darius said, leaning into the phone. "I told him Christmas day I wanted to marry his daughter."

"Christmas day? It's July. What took you so long?" Michelle asked.

"Your father didn't give me his blessing until last month. He said, 'Fine, take her,'" Darius said teasing.

"Yeah, sure. No way would my father say that. I'm the apple of his eye. Do you hear this man, Ma?"

She chuckled. "I hear him, baby. We know better."

"Okay, Ma, I'll talk with you later. I have to call the girls."

"Congratulations, baby. I'm so happy for you," she said.

Michelle clicked off the call and phoned Shianne.

"Hey girl, what's happening?" Shianne asked.

"I'm what's happening," Michelle said, her voice filled with emotion. "Darius and I are what's happening. We're getting married!"

"Darius asked you to marry him?"

"Yes."

Shianne let out an excited shriek. "When did he ask you?"

"A few moments ago."

Shianne shrieked again. "Put Darius on the phone."

"I'll put him on speaker."

"Congratulations, my friend. It's about time you popped the question. I'm so happy for you two. You'll make a great husband for my bestie."

"Thanks. That's my plan. I knew I had to have her after our first date."

"I think she fell for you then too," Shianne said, chuckling.

"Hey, wifey-to-be, it's closing time. Why don't you and Darius come to the bakery and have champagne pastries with us."

"Champagne pastries? Aren't you ready to go home?"

"Come on. It'll be fun. We'll have everything ready by the time you get here. Have you told Erica?"

"I was calling her next."

"So, are you coming?"

Michelle smiled and looked at Darius.

"I'm game," he said.

"We'll see you guys within the hour," Michelle said.

She and Darius were beside themselves with joy and relaxed at his house for a while, having a champagne moment alone before heading to the bakery.

CHAPTER TWENTY-FOUR

Shianne, Chef Brown, and Frederick worked feverishly to put together a celebratory party that would wow the soon-to-be bride and groom. Champagne cupcakes with dark chocolate buttercream frosting, assorted sorbet sundaes with the bubbly, strawberry champagne trifles, and cake puffs displayed on a beautifully decorated dessert table. Caramelized onions and parmesan cheese puff squares, mini chicken salad sandwiches stuffed with mushrooms, and mozzarella cheese sliders displayed at another table.

Michelle and Darius strode into the bakery hand in hand.

"So I guess congratulations are in order," Gregory said, opening his arms widely and embracing Michelle.

He then faced Darius, shaking his hand. "Congrats, man. So, she said yes?"

Darius smiled brilliantly. "Yes!"

"It's time to celebrate," Gregory said, lowering the window shades.

Shianne ran up to Michelle and let out a screech. Michelle outstretched her hand to show off her ring.

"Ooh, that's beautiful. Gorgeous. Simply lovely. You have to tell me everything. I want every detail!" She took Michelle's elbow and led her to the dessert table.

"Had he given you any hint that he was going to ask you to marry him?"

"No. Not at all. I wasn't expecting it."

Michelle marveled at the pastries as they neared the table. "Wow! I should get engaged more often."

"Anything for you, my friend." Shianne wrapped her arm around Michelle.

A moment later, Chef Brown brought out a champagne bottle and was about to pop the cork when Erica and Paul arrived. All eyes turned on them.

"Congratulations, cousin," Paul said, hugging Michelle tightly. "It looks like Darius is the man, after all."

"I didn't know you were in town," Michelle said.

"I came in yesterday."

"Yesterday! And you didn't tell me you were here? Are you here on business?"

Erica wrapped her arm around his shoulder. "Yes. I'm his business. He's here to see me."

Michelle was speechless.

"But it's not about Paul and me right now," Erica said. "Congratulations, girl! Let me see your ring."

Michelle extended her hand for display.

"Whoa! Now that's a head-turner. It's jaw-droppingly gorgeous." She smiled at Darius.

"I had to bring my A-game," Darius said, stepping toward them. "I searched for a while for that ring."

Erica smiled widely. "I bet you did."

She faced Paul. "Honey, will you look at this ring? It's stunning."

Paul viewed the ring. "It's nice, cousin. Very nice."

"We'll talk later," Michelle whispered in Paul's ear. "We have some talking to do."

Chef Brown poured champagne into everyone's glass, and Shianne raised her glass of sparkling water. "Here's to Michelle and Darius, a divine couple I wish nothing but the best."

"Cheers!" the group said in unison.

The girls then sat at a table and chatted. "So much happened today that I never expected Darius would ask me to marry him," Michelle said.

"What do you mean?" Shianne asked. "What happened today?"

"Carolyn happened. We watched DJ this afternoon, and when she returned, she acted a total witch.

Erica shook her head. "Poor thing. Just can't let it go."

"She threatened not to let Darius see DJ."

Erica gasped and put down her cupcake. "I know she didn't!"

"Darius told her she'd better get used to seeing me around because we were getting married. And this was before he asked me to marry him."

Erica bristled. "Sounds like things got a little hot over there. That's what she gets. I should rub it in her face that you and Darius are getting married. I'll tell her she brought out the best in Darius."

"Nah, don't do that, girl. She's already hurting." She paused. "Let's not spoil this day talking about Carolyn."

"I guess you're right," Erica said and took a sip of champagne.

Shianne looked at the girls and smiled. "You know, all of us have gone through some changes this year, me opening the bakery and getting pregnant, you getting engaged, Michelle." She turned to Erica. "And what's up with you and Paul?"

"Yeah, what's going on with you two?" Michelle asked. "He didn't even let me know he was coming to town. I know he said he came yesterday, but how long has he been here?"

Erica looked upward for a moment as if the answer would fall from the ceiling.

"Girl, how long has he been here?" Michelle asked impatiently.

"Since Wednesday."

"Four days? He's been here four days, and you guys didn't call anyone or say anything?" Michelle said. "What have you done to my cousin? You've corrupted him!"

Erica gazed at Chef Brown, who was pouring champagne, and raised her glass, indicating she wanted more of the bubbly.

Chef Brown stepped to the table and poured, and Erica immediately took two sips.

"Okay, as you know, Paul and I have had feelings for each other for a while, but we couldn't get it together. We've decided to try it one more time, and, if it fails, there's no turning back. We're through. We've been talking every day since my pregnancy scare. He was disappointed I wasn't pregnant."

"Aw," Michelle said.

"So, Aaron is completely out of the picture?" Shianne asked.

"Yes. Aaron is gone." She took another sip of champagne. "Paul and I have decided that I would move to Portland. He has the most to lose by moving here. I plan to join him in a few months."

"You're moving in with him?" Shianne asked.

"No, I'm getting a place."

"Well, I'm happy for you guys. I hope you can make it work this time," Michelle said.

"Me too," Shianne added.

"I'm still mad at Paul for not telling me he was coming," Michelle said.

Shianne laughed. "Girl, get over it. You have more important things to concentrate on, like that stunning dress you'll be wearing on your wedding day."

"Yes, that does take precedence over Paul."

"I can't wait for us to go shopping," Shianne said.

Michelle smiled. "Yeah, it'll be too much fun!"

"Let's start looking next week," Erica said. "Have you set a date?"

"Soon," Darius said, walking over to Michelle and kissing her. "As far as I'm concerned, we can get married tomorrow."

"Tomorrow?" the girls exclaimed.

"It won't be tomorrow, but maybe in September," Michelle said.

"That is soon, but we can roll with it. Right, Shianne?" Erica asked.

"Yes, because I'm expected to deliver the baby in October."

CHAPTER TWENTY-FIVE

Bakery

"Michelle, come on out here, girl. This is the seventeenth dress you've tried on. I'm tired, and I'm hungry," Erica said, looking into the empty bag of Chex Mix she had been eating from all morning. She turned to Shianne. "I know you're ready to eat. You're eating for two."

"Yes, I'm starving," she said, handing her plastic bag of raisins and nuts to Erica.

Shianne tried to be patient. She knew finding the most beautiful wedding dress in the world takes time. It had taken her several weeks before she had found her wedding dress. It was their third time shopping with Michelle for a dress.

Shianne briefed Erica on the goings-on between her and Miles as they waited. She and Miles had let the girls get together for a sleepover at Shianne's the past weekend.

Shianne smiled. "They had a good time together. They didn't go to bed until past midnight."

"Maybe they will like each other enough to call each other 'play sister' one day, "Erica said.

Shianne shrugged. "I don't know. I wish I had a crystal ball to see how things will work out."

Inside the dressing room, Michelle stood in front of a large mirror, fascinated. "Oh, I love this dress. It's beautiful," she said of the ivory off-the-shoulder flare gown with beaded Venice lace. She pulled back the silk curtain for her girls to see.

Shianne's eyes widened. "Oh, my goodness. What a beautiful dress!"

"It's gorgeous," Erica said. "I love it. It looks awesome on you. It's the Michelle dress."

"Isn't it beautiful?" Michelle turned around to give a full view of the dress. "I felt it in my spirit this morning that I'd find my dress today." She exhaled a deep breath.

"Girl, you look stunning." Shianne exhaled. "It's breathtaking."

Michelle stood in front of the mirror for several moments, admiring the dress. She then twirled excitedly. "This is it! This is the dress!"

She took off the dress moments later and helped the girls find their bridesmaid dresses. More than an hour passed before Shianne fell in love with a lovely rose one-shoulder floor-length chiffon dress, and Erica a rose, off-the-shoulder asymmetrical dress.

"I hope I can get into this dress in a few months," Shianne said.

"You'll be fine. You've ordered it a few sizes larger, and you heard the seamstress say she has extra fabric on hand if she needs to do her magic," Michelle said.

Shianne sighed. "Okay, let's eat! I'm starving."

"Me too," Erica said.

"I'm buying," Michelle said. "You ladies can order whatever you want."

Shianne licked her lips. "I have a taste for salmon, chicken tacos, and a chopped salad."

"Is that all?" Michelle asked, laughing.

"For now."

"You didn't mention your favorite eggs and peppers sprinkled with chocolate," Erica chimed.

Michelle moaned. "Icky."

"It's delicious. You have to try it."

"You couldn't pay me to eat that stuff."

Shianne shrugged and started walking down the street, with Michelle and Erica following.

The girls settled at a restaurant a few blocks from the bridal shop and helped Michelle further plan her wedding. Shianne was the matron of honor, and Erica, the maid of honor. Kaiya and Darius's nephew, Marcus, would be the flower girl and ring bearer. Darius had already selected his oldest brother, Keith, as his best man.

Michelle smiled. "Now, all I need to do is reserve the church and banquet hall, and finish the wedding invitations."

Erica tapped her on the arm. "I love your invitations. They're so elegant," she said of the boysenberry and silver invites.

"I make greeting cards for Christ's sake. I'd better be able to come up with a spectacular card for my wedding."

"I love the picture of you and Darius," Shianne said.

"Darius's cousin, Thomas, took it. He's the photographer for the wedding also."

"Well, all right now," Shianne said, smiling as she put the last batch of eggs in her mouth. "Mm, that was good!"

Michelle shook her head. "I can't believe you ate that."

Michelle's face glowed, having found her wedding gown. She almost knocked Darius down from excitement when she answered the door. "I found my dress! I found my dress!"

He grinned. "I thought you were thrilled to see me, but it's great you've found a dress. So, tell me about it," he said, taking her hand and walking further into the house.

Michelle dove right in describing every detail of the gown, gushing between sentences. "I'm going to look so beautiful!"

"I'm sure you'll make that dress look beautiful, baby."

CHAPTER TWENTY-SIX

Michelle couldn't believe her eyes when she spotted Brandon in the bookstore.

No, no, no. Damn!

Michelle wished she could have clicked her heels and been home. Instead, she stood in line, hoping the customers before her would hurry with their purchases. She turned her face from him, pretending to be reading the book she was buying.

"Hey, Michelle," he said, stepping up to her.

She exhaled a deep sigh. "Hey."

"How are you?" He flashed the smile that at one time had warmed her heart.

"I'm fine."

He reached out to hug her, but Michelle stepped away. He shifted his body back and forth. "Funny running into you here."

"No one expects to run into anyone when they're out, they just do."

He gazed at the book she was holding. "Stagecoach Mary?"

"Yes. The girls and I were talking about her recently, and I thought I'd read up on her."

"Wasn't she the first black woman to carry the mail?"

Michelle nodded, glancing at the line that had not moved. The customer at the register was rummaging through her handbag for her credit card.

Michelle spied the book he was buying by First Lady Michelle Obama. He lifted his hand, showing her the cover.

"Today's Mom's birthday, and since she loves Michelle so much, I thought I'd buy it for her."

"How is your mother?"

A grin crossed his lips. "Mom's doing well. She asks about you all the time."

Hearing his mother ask about her made Michelle smile inside. She adored Brandon's mother and had looked forward to her being her mother-in-law one day. "Well, tell her I said happy birthday."

He nodded. "I will."

Michelle and Brandon had met at a Kem concert in Chicago and immediately became friends after learning they both had attended Howard University. They chuckled at the what-ifs had they met at school, and their romance had followed shortly after.

Michelle sighed with relief as it came time for her to pay for her book. She handed the clerk her credit card but regretted it as the seconds dragged on, thinking cash would have gone much quicker.

"Well, nice seeing you, Brandon," she said, grabbing her receipt and talking to him as if he were an old friend and not a former lover. Michelle snatched her bag and rushed from the store, thinking she'd be gone by the time Brandon left the store. She hurried to her car and was about to drive off when Brandon tapped her window and gestured for her to let it down.

Damn, what does he want now?

She pressed the button, and the window opened. "What's up?"

"I was wondering if we could get together and talk while I'm here. I'll be here for a week. I want to discuss what happened between us." He shifted from side to side. "Things ended badly between us, Michelle. There were too many loose ends. I owe you an explanation."

"No, you don't. There's nothing to explain. It is what it is."

"How can you act so smug? You act as if we had nothing. We were in love with each other. I still love you."

A distraught look crossed her face. "How can you expect me to be so accommodating when you cheated on me? You lied to me. You brought your girlfriend home for a night of sex, not expecting I would be there." She breathed. "I bet you wish you hadn't given me a key. You looked as if I were the second coming when you guys came into the bedroom." Michelle shook her head as if dismissing that night.

"Things were working as planned. I was getting things ready for you to join me in Minnesota."

She grew agitated. "So that woman who was rushing behind you to your bedroom was a figment of my imagination?"

Brandon swallowed deep. "I'm sorry, Michelle. I hurt today, thinking about how I messed things up for us. A group of us had gotten together to celebrate a coworker's birthday that night, and I'd had too much to drink."

She tapped the steering wheel with her fingertips. "Oh, so the alcohol made you want to get with your coworker? They say drinking only gives you the courage to do the things you want to do."

"No, but … I didn't have any feelings for her. Things just happened."

"If I hadn't been there, would things have proceeded to happen?"

He crossed his arms and stood silent. His face appeared pained.

"Are you with her now?"

"Why didn't you answer my calls when I reached out to you?"

"So, you're asking a question with a question?"

"I just wanted to talk to you. Say I was sorry."

For several weeks after their split, Brandon had called and had pleaded for Michelle to take him back. "*I know I did wrong. I'm sorry. Please forgive me. I don't want to lose you. I'm blessed to have you in my life,*" the messages had repeated.

Looking slightly annoyed, Michelle said, "I didn't want to hear any of your excuses. I didn't want to hear your lies. You did what you did. Own up to it."

Brandon exhaled a deep sigh.

"Well, it's water under the bridge, Brandon. I have to get going. My fiancé and I are going to the car show this afternoon," she lied.

He cocked his head. "Fiancé?"

"Yes, I'm getting married. Life didn't end when we broke up, Brandon."

He stepped backward and put his hand over his heart. "Whoa, that stung. I figured you would be with someone, but getting married? It's hard hearing you say this. When are you getting married?"

"Why does it matter?"

"I was just wondering." Brandon stood silent for a few moments. "I know it doesn't matter now, but I came to town when Aunt Vi died. I drove to your house and sat outside for hours."

"You knew she had died?"

"Yes, Mom told me."

Michelle had wanted to hear from him during that time. Aunt Vi's death had devastated her, and despite support from family and friends, she had wanted him there. He never showed.

"I needed you, Brandon. You knew how much I loved my aunt. I swore I'd never speak to you again after you didn't show up."

"I'm sorry, but I didn't think you wanted to see me."

"Then why did you park outside my house?"

He stood silent for a moment. "Do you love him?"

"Yes. Yes. Of course, I love him."

She could see the hurt in his eyes.

"You might not want to hear it, but I think about you all the time." He fidgeted. "Do you ever think about me? I know it's not as easy as you make it appear. You loved me too."

"Yes, I did love you but now I love someone else."

Brandon stood silent for several moments before saying, "Thanks for hearing me out. I was hoping I'd run into you somewhere."

"And you did," she retorted, feeling resentment welling in her body.

"I've never stopped loving you, Michelle."

She cut her eyes at him and said nothing.

"Take care of yourself," he said moments later. He tapped the car door as if giving her permission to leave.

"You too," she said and drove away.

Michelle had hoped for closure with Brandon but having had "the talk" she felt it wasn't as important as she had thought. Brandon was the first man she had truly loved, and before meeting Darius, she might have gone back to him. But she had met Darius. He was her saving grace.

CHAPTER TWENTY-SEVEN

Bakery

Michelle had been awake for more than an hour, her mind crisscrossing between the wedding and Darius. She smiled, thinking about the first time she and Darius had met, and then meeting for dinner weeks later. She closed her eyes and prayed aloud.

"Father God, thank you for this day. Thank you for this wonderful man I'm marrying. Please bless our marriage. May we grow stronger in you. Darius will be a great husband. I pray for the grace to be the wife he needs."

Within moments, a chime from her cell rang, alerting her to a text. Michelle picked up her phone from the nightstand and read.

Good morning, baby. I woke up feeling incredibly happy knowing that you'll be my wife and lying in my arms this time tomorrow. I thank God for you, Michelle! I love you so much that it hurts. See you soon, beautiful.

"Aw, so sweet," Michelle said to herself. She responded.

Darius, you're everything I've wanted and prayed for in a man. You're the best boyfriend a girl can have, and I know you will be a better husband. I lay here praying for us and smiling like a child with candy because I will wake up beside you every morning. Your love is addictive. See you in moments.

Michelle wiped away a stray tear and lay there thinking a few moments before getting into the shower. She then put on one of Darius's T-shirts and headed downstairs, treading lightly as not to awaken Erica, who had spent the night.

To her surprise, Erica was at the table, sipping a cup of coffee. "I expected you up an hour ago, wifey-to-be," Erica said, smiling.

"I've been up for a while. I was lying in bed, thinking."

Michelle poured a cup of coffee and sat in a chair across from her. "Thank God it's stopped raining."

"I saw a rainbow outside my window this morning. They say rain on your wedding day is a sign of good luck," Erica said.

Michelle smiled. "So they say." She glanced at the bowl of fresh fruit on the table.

"I didn't know if you wanted to eat anything, especially since we ate so much last night," Erica said.

"Shianne cooked up some food, didn't she? I don't know why she cooked so much! It was just Mama and us." The ladies had gotten together at Michelle's following a day at the spa.

"It was her way of showing you love. You know that. The chef extraordinaire is so happy for you, and so am I."

Erica tossed a grape inside her mouth, and through chews, asked, "Are you nervous? Because I sure am."

Michelle laid down her mug. "Come on now! Only one of us should be nervous, and that's me."

Michelle rested her chin on her palm. "Life never works out the way you plan it. I thought I'd marry Brandon but in a matter of hours I'll be marrying someone else."

Erica nodded. "Girl, don't I know. Look at me and Paul. I never thought we would get back together after our last breakup. Let alone even speak to each other again. We said some very hurtful things to each other. But we slowly became friends again, and we're in a very good space right now. I've grown. He's grown. And so has our love for each other."

"I'm rooting for you guys again. Paul is a good man."

Erica smiled. "That's why I'm willing to give us another try."

The doorbell rang interrupting their talk.

"Either that's Shianne or our glam squad," Michelle said.

Erica went to the door. It was Shianne along with the hair and makeup stylists.

A few hours later, Michelle, Shianne, and Erica was all dolled up and on their way to Ebenezer Baptist Church in a white stretch limousine.

"I feel fabulous," Michelle said, getting into the limo.

"You look beautiful," Shianne said.

"And so do you ladies."

A half-hour later the girls walked inside the church. Michelle took a deep breath, overwhelmed by the sanctuary's beauty. Winding greenery housing gardenias, calla lilies, orchids, and ranunculus flowers made a statement at each pew. The girls strolled down the aisle where a wedding arch adorned with lights wowed them, just like Michelle had imagined.

"Simply gorgeous," Shianne said, holding her hand.

"It's lovely," Michelle said softly, holding back tears.

"I was going to joke and say you have less than an hour to change your mind, but your face says it all," Shianne said.

Within moments, they heard the sound of men's voices. "Sounds like the groom is here," Erica said. She took Michelle's hand and giggled. "Let's get you out of here; I don't want Darius forgetting his name before the ceremony."

The girls then went inside a room adjacent to the sanctuary and relaxed until the wedding ceremony began.

"Looks like I made the right decision about the dress size," Shianne said, viewing herself in the mirror.

"You look so pretty," Michelle said.

"Thanks. I've been nervous about not getting into this dress. I've gained five pounds this week alone. I still have three more weeks to go!"

"Well, no worries today," Michelle said as the hairstylist, who had met the girls at the church, spritzed her updo.

Moments later there was a tap on the door. "Come out, baby, it's time," Mr. Anthony's deep voice rang out.

Michelle's eyes widened as she looked at the girls. She took a deep breath. "Okay, Daddy, we'll be out in a minute." She looked at Erica. "You're supposed to keep us on track."

"I know, but we were talking."

"Great bridesmaids we are," Shianne said, smiling.

The stylists gave the girls one last look over, and Shianne stepped toward the door first. Michelle kissed Shianne and Erica on the cheek before they stepped out of the room. Michelle followed moments later.

"You're beautiful, baby," Mr. Anthony said. He took her hand and escorted her into the church. Her eyes filled with tears upon seeing Darius.

"Welcome, family, friends, and loved ones of Darius Mathews and Michelle Anthony," Reverend Timothy Marks opened.

Shianne hadn't said anything, but she'd felt sick all morning. The thought of her delivering her baby during the ceremony terrified her. They were well into the wedding ceremony when Shianne felt a small gush of warm water trickle down her legs. She had felt dampness in her underwear during the processional, but she put it out of her mind.

Within moments, a sharp pain struck her belly causing a light moan. Her heart raced. She looked at Gregory, whose eyes were on Michelle. She then faced Michelle, who was tearing up as she exchanged her vows with Darius.

Though in pain, Shianne made it through the nuptials. It was a beautiful ceremony, but to Shianne, every moment was agony. Her body heated, and sweat beaded on her forehead. Gregory looked over at her when Reverend Marks pronounced Darius and Michelle man and wife. She mouthed, "Let's go."

"Are you having contractions, baby?" he asked when they reached the vestibule.

"Yes. I had a strong contraction a few minutes ago."

"Let's get you to the hospital." Gregory took her hand, and they headed toward the door.

"Where are you two going?" Erica asked.

"The hospital. I think I'm in labor," Shianne said. "We'll call you guys later."

Erica's eyes widened. "Should I come with?"

"No, you stay here with Michelle. We'll call from the hospital."

"Are you sure?"

"Girl, yes," Shianne said, and she and Gregory left the church.

Through all the excitement, Michelle hadn't noticed Shianne and Gregory had left the church. "Where's Shianne? I want to take some pictures at the church before we go to the reception."

Erica swallowed. "She's gone to the hospital. She and Gregory left right after the ceremony. She thought she was in labor."

"What? Why didn't someone tell me?"

"You were busy with your wedding, Michelle. They're going to keep us posted."

"Jesus?" Michelle stared at her as if she had lost her mind. "Okay, but as soon as you hear something let me know."

"I will. Now, go and enjoy yourself."

A few hours passed before Erica received Gregory's call. Shianne was in labor but doctors expected it would be several hours before she delivered. Erica immediately got the news to Michelle and Darius.

"We talked about something like this happening," Michelle said, shaking her head.

As they talked, the DJ called Michelle and Darius to the floor for their special dance. He took her hand and led her to the middle of the floor. Chrisette Michele's "A Couple of Forevers" played.

Darius wrapped his arms around Michelle. "What a day, huh?"

She nodded and smiled. "Yes, What a day!"

He then looked lovingly into her eyes and said, "I'm so happy, baby. I couldn't wait for this day to come. I got the girl of my dreams."

"I could scream from the mountaintops!" Michelle said, holding him closer. "Looks like I'm that classy, sassy, woman after all."

Darius smiled. "I knew you were all the time."

"Darius... Darius, someone is knocking at the door," Michelle said.

He didn't respond.

"Darius," Michelle repeated, shoving him lightly. "Honey, please get the door."

"Okay," he said, slowing climbing out of bed and throwing on his robe. He walked sluggishly to the door and answered.

"Good morning, Mr. Mathews, someone requested a six a.m. wake-up call," the hotel clerk said. "Well, it's six o'clock." He handed Darius a tray containing hot coffee and pastries. "Have a great day."

"Thanks, man," Darius said, closing the door. Darius placed the tray on a table and poured coffee into a cup, and sipped. "Michelle, it's time to get up."

She didn't answer.

He walked over to the bed and sat beside her. "Good morning, baby. It's time to get up. Dominica is calling us." He kissed her on the cheek.

Michelle looked at him with one eye open. "It's six o'clock already?"

"Yes, baby," he answered, holding the coffee before her.

"It seems like we just went to bed, babe."

Darius smiled.

"That coffee smells wonderful," Michelle said, taking in the aroma. She sat upright and reached for the cup.

"You enjoy your coffee, and I'll shower first," Darius said, stepping away.

Several minutes afterward, Darius returned, and Michelle took her shower. The two dressed and were in the limousine by seven. Knowing they would pass the hospital on the way to the airport, Michelle suggested they run into the hospital and visit Shianne and the baby for a few minutes.

"Okay, but we have to hurry, Michelle. We can't miss our flight."

"We'll run in and say hello and leave. I promise you."

Arriving at the hospital fifteen minutes later, Michelle and Darius raced to the maternity ward.

"Hello, I'm Michelle Anthony. I mean Michelle Mathews, and we're here to see Shianne White," she said winded.

The nurse smiled. "Mrs. White mentioned you might show up here. She's breastfeeding the baby. I'll show you where to wash your hands, and then I'll take you to her room."

"I'll wait for you, baby," Darius said. "Tell them I said congratulations!"

Michelle stepped into the room moments later. Shianne lay in bed holding baby Thomas. Gregory sat at their side.

"Hey!" Michelle whispered. "I had to see the baby before we left for our honeymoon." She strolled over to the bed. "Aw, he's so cute. He looks like you, Gregory, but he has Shianne's eyes."

Shianne smiled. "Something told me you'd be showing up. I hate I missed the reception, but Thomas . . . My water burst during the ceremony!"

Michelle's eyes grew large. "Why didn't you say something?"

"What was I supposed to say? 'I'm in labor, everybody. Got to go.'"

"Yes!" Michelle said, shaking her head.

"The wedding ceremony was beautiful," Shianne said. "Where's Darius?"

"He's in the waiting room. He told me to tell you and Gregory congratulations!"

"Tell him we send our congratulations." She smiled. "God is so good. Just think we can celebrate your wedding anniversary and Thomas's birthday on the same day. That's going to be so much fun."

Michelle looked at baby Thomas. "He's so cute and chubby. Erica said he weighs over nine pounds!"

"He's nine pounds seven ounces."

"It's no wonder all the crap you ate." She turned to Gregory. "Who eats eggs with green peppers and chocolate?"

He chuckled lightly. "Crazy, right? But actually, it's not that bad. I was eating my eggs that way by the end of her pregnancy."

Michelle moaned and shook her head. "Both of you are crazy."

Shianne and Michelle regarded each other, tears welling in their eyes. "Well, you've seen the baby. Vamoose! Monte Plata is waiting for you, Mrs. Mathews. You and your hubby have a fantastic time."

Michelle kissed Shianne's forehead and then said, "Love you."

"Love you too. We'll see you and Darius in two weeks."

"I'll check on the bakery when I get back. See if Chef Brown needs my help," Michelle said, walking toward the door.

Shianne grinned. "I'm not going to respond to that."

Michelle chuckled and waved goodbye.

The End

ABOUT THE AUTHOR

A former journalist, DeVon Nelson, published her first romance novel
— *The Bitter and Sweet Around Me* — in 2011. Since then, she has self-
published three romance novels, *Bitter Can Taste Oh So Sweet, Gotta Find
My Way Back*, which received a nomination for Outstanding Achievement
in Literature from the African American Arts Alliance of Chicago, and her
new novel, *A Bakery Called Scrumptious.*

Born in Waukegan, Ill., - the setting for her first novel — DeVon earned
her B.A. from Southern Illinois University, Carbondale, Ill., where she
majored in journalism. She has over a decade of writing for the News-Sun
in Waukegan, Il., and the Chicago Tribune.

When she's not reading or writing romance stories, she's playing with her
nephews Legend, Zavonn, Skylar, and Xavion, learning how to blog, or
cooking up a big pot of spaghetti.

You can follow her using the below links:

facebook.com/DeVon-Publishing-1157190277655853

twitter.com/fdevon7